BASED ON A T

TEARS IN THE FLAG

SIDDHARTH BINDRA

outskirts
press

Outskirts Press, Inc.
http://www.outskirtspress.com

Paperback ISBN: 978-1-9772-3183-3
Hardback ISBN: 978-1-9772-3302-8

Outskirts Press and the "OP" logo are trademarks belonging to Outskirts Press, Inc.

PRINTED IN THE UNITED STATES OF AMERICA

FOREWORD

A raw, heart rendering story of lived experience as opposed to observed experience, Tears in the Flag, is an autobiographical journey through the eyes of a young Indian immigrant whose family is seeking the promise of the American Dream only to be confronted by the reality of a broken, and far too often, unjust immigration system. Overcoming all odds, our Protagonist, Arjun, becomes an American citizen in 2014, but not before enduring a harrowing and tear-filled, 15-year journey in order to get there.

Separation of family is a situation all too often faced by immigrants coming to this country. Arjun and his sister were forced to grow up without their deported mother, brought up by a father constantly beaten down by the system as he tries to build a life for his family in America. Lonely, and feeling like "the other," Arjun is able to find a few friends and confidants to help sustain him. His compassion toward others, especially family, and the passion that he displays for love and life also help him to survive and eventually thrive.

The story is filled with the images of history, Bollywood films, and literature that encompasses the popular culture and the historical promise that help sustain Arjun as he moves forward despite the overwhelming obstacles thrown his way. What Arjun manages to accomplish in his educational and business pursuits is nothing short of miraculous.

The timeliness of this book is on target, in the current U. S. political atmosphere, in which the executive branch of the government is using immigrants as pawns in a political game, and as a daughter of an Indian immigrant is elevated to the position of a Vice Presidential candidate for a major political party. It is a must read for those trying to understand the immigrant experience from the inside. As I read the book, it was as if I could feel and see, first hand, what Arjun and his family were experiencing.

For Sid, not only was the writing of this story cathartic; he hopes that by sharing the story more widely he will help those who may find themselves in similar circumstances. More importantly, Sid hopes that the readers will see the reality of what the system can do to an individual and a family as they chase the ever-elusive American Promise. Too often, those privileged not to have lived Sid's experience, see the faceless immigrants as numbers, just one of many who come here as a result of the pull of America's Promise. We believe they are fortunate to be here and are being given an equal opportunity to succeed. Nothing could be further from the truth. The playing field, even if they are allowed on it, is anything but equal.

To overcome such odds and become a highly successful financial adviser with a major institution is not just a credit to our Protagonist. It is a credit to generations of immigrants who have come here seeking the American Dream, and once experiencing it, have worked to make that dream more accessible to future generation of immigrants. Sid is clearly paying it forward after having paid so many tears for the right to do so.

Joel T. Jenne, PhD

TABLE OF CONTENTS

Chapter 1

July 15, 2002

Our life's journey is determined by a few pivotal moments, the ones we can never forget a single detail of, the ones that will forever change who we are meant to become. This was my moment. I was getting off the school bus and making my way to my aunt's townhome in the Baytree neighborhood of Dover, Delaware, where my mother had been staying as she recovered from her gallbladder removal surgery a few days ago. When I arrived, I saw Mom and Dad with packed suitcases in our silver Ford Windstar. There was a panicked look on Mom's face. Dad's face didn't give up any expression, but something clearly big was happening. Just a week before, an immigration officer had made his way to my aunt's place in an attempt to verify a pending USCIS (United States Citizenship and Immigration Services) case. The case, which had been filed in 2000, was for an adjustment in status for permanent residency based on marriage to a US citizen. That US citizen and petitioner was my aunt, whom we called Masi, and the application was for my dad; my younger sister, Sonya; and me to become green card holders. The "paper marriage"

1

between Masi and Dad was our path to citizenship, and the thought process was that it would go through without any hiccup. The petition could only include the spouse of the US citizen and their children, so Mom couldn't be part of the filing. It was more important for her husband, the breadwinner of the family, and her children to become legal first—she could wait her turn.

Well, the hiccup happened when the interview did not result in an approval. I remember the awkward moment in the interview room as I sat behind Dad and Masi. This process was meant to determine the validity of their marriage, presented as a second marriage after divorce. But divorces are quite rare in Indian culture, and add in four children—two from Dad's side and two from Masi's—and the story becomes more unconvincing. The case was put on pending status, and everyone went back to their lives as if it would just be a matter of time before the green cards magically showed up. They didn't, but the immigration officer did two years later when he knocked on our door, and he did his best to make sure the case was legitimate. The scenario played out like the movie *The Proposal* with Sandra Bullock and Ryan Reynolds, where a creepy immigration officer follows the newlywed couple to Alaska at the request of Ryan's rich dad to investigate the legitimacy of the marriage. When things look shady, people usually check up on their hunches. My aunt's townhouse was filled with traces of the people who lived there but not one picture of my dad or us. The three bedrooms in the house were made up of the master bedroom, where my aunt and grandmother slept, and the other two belonged to my cousins, Hardeep and Amanjot. There were no clothes in the closets that belonged to a grown man or a total of four children. Basically, it was set up in the exact manner that was intended—without us in it.

As a twelve-year-old, I had no say in the matter, and as a thirty-year-old man now, it's hard to fathom the thought process and actions of these adults that would come to shape the shaky foundation years of our lives in America. These adults were all responsible for what occurred. They didn't plan for the worst, and the worst happened. During the time the case had been applied for up to the day the officer came, everything that could have been done wrongly was done, out of either ignorance or plain disregard for the system. The documents requested by the Immigration and Naturalization Services (INS), later known as the Department of Homeland Security (DHS), were printed out from a Microsoft Word document composed by yours truly at the direction of my father. What happened next should have come as no surprise to all who were involved—but everyone was still dumbfounded. I remember the moment I saw the man who would forever change our lives as I stood on the second level in our three-story townhouse. I was afraid, but I couldn't say a word or it could jeopardize the investigation. I acted the part and tried to blend in as a permanent resident of 500 Schooner Way, but it was pointless. Dad panicked and decided to show the immigration officer around the townhouse where no evidence of us living there existed. Then he followed up this action by taking the officer to our apartment unit just a little bit down the road in the same neighborhood. The officer knocked on the door, and my mom, scared out of her mind, refused to open it, her thought being that this was it—they are going to arrest us all and put us in orange jumpsuits and ship us off back to India.

As far as I could remember, my father was always a tough man. Most of the memories I have of him from childhood were terrifying. For an Indian man, he had a larger physique than almost everyone else, and he ruled our household with a heavy hand. I remember literally pissing myself on multiple occasions when I would receive routine beatings. Think of a strict parent in the 1960s—that was my Dad. He carried himself as a strong personality type, but he was strong only against those he could intimidate with his words and his size. When things started falling apart, he was just as lost as anyone else.

Masi, my mother's sister, was a tall, attractive, prideful, and independent woman with a strong personality that resembled that of her mother, Bibi. Masi had had an arranged marriage to a man named Kuljeet Singh, who was almost a decade older than her. He was an NRI (nonresident Indian) of America who had served some time in the armed forces and was a US citizen. He was quite wealthy in America as a business owner and had family money in India. The trend of NRI marriages in the villages of Punjab, where parents married their daughters off to receive a better life in America, was quite popular in the early 1990s. The attraction of America was too good to pass up even if it meant sending your child a world away. No wonder Bibi came to America around this time when Masi's marriage was ending to help her raise her children; there must have been some sense of guilt that she couldn't be there for her child when she was in pain. During their divorce proceedings in 1997, Masi refused to lay a claim on half of his wealth, which would have been close to a million dollars or more. In her words: "He spent his entire life building this; I won't just take it from him." Instead, she settled for a meager sum of fifty thousand dollars and child support.

Masi opted to stay in San Antonio, Texas, honoring joint custody of their children, living in an apartment complex fifteen minutes from her previous home. She and her ex-husband tried to make their relationship work again at some point in 1999. When things looked as though they could be resolved, Bibi left San Antonio to come and stay with us in Dover. A little while later, after my aunt and cousins had moved back in with her ex-husband in San Antonio, he unpredictably threw them out of his house. They spent some time staying with my aunt's friend, Lucky Aunty, in San Antonio before they flew to Dover. Coming to Dover to be near to us was the only logical option left for Masi after the traumatic end in San Antonio; we were the only family she had in America. Unknown to me, this move was also because of a legal petition filed two years before in a New Jersey courthouse where my Dad and Masi had gotten married a year and half after Masi left her ex-husband. They had listed their legal residence was in Dover, Delaware. Perhaps Masi's ex-husband had found out about this paper marriage; maybe he had even been responsible for filing an official complaint with the INS on the validity of the case.

In the early part of the new millennium, Masi purchased her townhouse in Dover, and in order for her to get approved for the loan without adding my dad's name on the deed, she marked her status as separated from her new husband. If both names had been added to the loan application, then both parties would have been joint owners on the deed of the new house, which Masi didn't want. All this happened in the middle of a pending immigration case, further evidence that these two people weren't genuinely married or had separated shortly after filing their immigration petition. At this point, they might as well have stood outside the INS office with a sign that said: "We are full of shit" and "This marriage isn't real." It wouldn't take Sherlock Holmes to unravel the complicated structure of this case; it was right there in front of everyone, and the result was deserved.

Things had changed dramatically after the 9/11 attacks in 2001, and the few months and years following the tragedy weren't the best time to be a brown person in America. Xenophobia was rampant, and our dark-olive skin tone looked similar to the skin color of the "new enemy." Everyone was afraid during a time that seemed like a bad dream. I remember being rushed out of school after the first tower was hit. Kids in the school hallways were talking about how a plane had crashed into the World Trade Center. I didn't even know what the World Trade Center was until we came home and turned on the news, where I saw the second plane hitting the building live. It's a memory from childhood that has been cemented in my mind, and one that any person might think would have been my most traumatic childhood memory. Maybe 9/11 was the reason why Mom thought we would be better off being with our own people in India than becoming the constant target of prejudice in America.

Fast forward to July 15, 2002, a week after the visit from the immigration officer. Once everything was packed, my mom rushed nine-year-old Sonya and me into the van, and so began our long car ride to JFK International Airport. It was never Dad's intention to leave with us as he truly believed things would work out in the end in America. He was as shaken as the rest of the family, but he wasn't ready to give up and run. Even when we reached New York and met with the agent who bought Mom's one-way ticket to India, he tried to convince the man to talk my mother out of her decision. She was being impulsive and irrational, and there was nothing to be so afraid of, he said. But there was no consoling my mother. There was no way she was going to let our failed attempt at gaining legal immigration status be the reason for her going to jail or being deported. She was going to leave by her own decision.

The pictures we took there that day have become infamous in the family. No matter how much Dad disagreed with her decision, he understood the significance of these events and purchased a disposable Kodak camera to capture the moment before our life would be shattered. There we all were in Terminal 1 of John F. Kennedy airport—my mother's expressionless face; Sonya, too young to realize what was happening; and me, trying to keep a brave face on, thinking everything would surely work out. The original plan had been for Mom, Sonya, and me to leave for India, but somewhere along the New Jersey Turnpike, Bibi had called and started pleading with Mom, trying to calm her down and beg her not to make a rash decision. Bibi kept saying "rab da vasta," which means "for God's sake."

"Think of your children," Bibi exclaimed. "You're uprooting their lives once again when they have just started to find some peace. Listen to me, beta, everything will be fine. You haven't done anything wrong to be so afraid. What is your crime? You are running away like you robbed a bank or killed a person. Stop and come back." When those pleas fell on deaf ears, Bibi convinced my mom to at least leave us kids behind. She didn't want my mother's fear of getting caught and being persecuted to be the reason we would be permanently banned from reentering America after overstaying our visas.

I felt like I had lost my ability to speak, and it was as if there were a giant stone sitting on my chest as I struggled to breathe. The unraveling of my parents' lives and our circumstances left me speechless. My fate was going to be decided by the people who were in the middle of a panic attack. But thank god for Bibi—my mom left alone. She had made her decision the moment the immigration officer knocked on our apartment door, and nothing was going to change her mind.

If I had known that I wouldn't see my mother again for more than a decade, I would have cried my eyes out and begged her not to leave. I was in shock, and I was afraid. I had never felt so helpless as when I roamed around the airport terminal, forgetting where I was or what was happening. Even though Sonya was so young, she would not let go of

Mom. Somehow, she understood more than me that we needed to make an effort to keep our mother with us. In the end, Mom hugged Sonya and me tightly before walking toward the security checkpoint, tears running down her face. She kept looking back, and we didn't move until we lost sight of her. I wish I had yelled loudly, "Mom, don't go!" But I did nothing. I do not even remember the car ride back home; it was as if everything after that moment stopped mattering. One has to wonder, did my mom know at the time that this would be the beginning of thirteen-plus years of exile? To be accurate, it would be thirteen years, five months, and four days before my mom would return to us in America, and what happened during that time sets the foundation for this story.

CHAPTER 2

IN INDIA, MY father was a banker or some sort of manager at the Bank of Punjab branch in Karnal, Haryana. I knew that we were doing quite well when I was growing up, which was all that mattered to me. When we used to visit our family in Patiala, which was about six hours northwest from Karnal, I knew we were well-to-do in comparison to the rest of the family. The perception of children is just as keen as an adult's when it comes to issues of wealth and class.

My family was Sikh in a country where 81 percent of the population was Hindu. Sikhism is a monotheistic religion based on the principle of one God, rejecting claims that any particular religious tradition has a monopoly on absolute truth. After persecution from the Mughals and the execution of two Sikh gurus for refusing to convert to Islam, Guru Gobind Singh Ji triggered the founding of the Khalsa as an order to protect the freedom of conscience and religion. The most visual of these characteristics was never cutting one's hair. My parents named me Arjun, after Arjuna from *Mahabharata*. My school was the best one in the city, St. Theresa's convent school, a Catholic school. Needless to say I had a very diverse religious upbringing in a homogeneous country.

I was six or so when my dad started traveling outside of India—his own version of the pursuit of happiness. Our family friends in Karnal who were looking to emigrate to the UK had received their UK visas quite easily, and they left for London shortly afterward. Dad followed suit. He was gone for six months and he came back unimpressed, or so one would think considering his next trip wasn't a return to the UK but to the grand prize itself, the United States of America. In 1995, Dad received his ten-year business visa and left for America in search of greener pastures. He would make this journey three more times before we would join him in the "land of the free" three years later in 1998.

My Dad was one of six children and the second youngest with an age difference of over ten years with his oldest sister. Dad was just a teenager when my frustrated paternal grandfather left his family, trying to put himself in faraway lands. I guess you could say my dad was doing a similar thing, but the difference was he always pulled his family along with him. Regardless of how short-tempered or discontented he was with his own situation, he always came back to bring his family along for the ride. This trend wasn't lost during the application process for our immigration case, when instead of applying for just himself, he put Sonya's and my name on the application as well. When he was in America by himself during his early thirties, he could have easily hustled and become a legal resident. I often wondered why he didn't selfishly take care of the problem then that, when left unresolved, would later ruin his life. Maybe he was stopped by the sense of betrayal to his marriage if he had gotten involved with someone in the US behind my mother's back in order to get his green card; maybe it was his resistance to follow a similar path to his father.

While my father was away, we continued with our lives in India, and things were always better whenever Bibi came to stay with us. She was my favorite grandparent, and I was utterly spoiled by her love. It wasn't that my other grandparents didn't love me; I just liked my Bibi the best. It also helped that I would see her the most, and her favoritism was evident. Whatever differences she had with my father, she never let me feel a hint of it. She always used to bring toys or gifts whenever she visited us and showered me with affection. My Dadi, or my Dad's mom, also loved me dearly, but she lived in an ashram for most of her life, devoted to seva and God. My paternal grandfather and my Dadi had split up decades before, but no one talked about it; it was taboo. My grandfather went on to travel the world and eventually settled in Dhaka, Bangladesh, where he met the love of his life.

In the first six or seven years of my life, I only recall two instances where I met my paternal grandfather, Bhagatt Singh. It's no wonder we didn't have an opportunity to build a relationship. The first time I ever met him, Dad was away in America. My grandfather had returned to India with his significant other who needed medical attention, and they visited us in Karnal. I remember riding in a rickshaw with my grandfather every day to the local hospital, where she was being treated. One day, as we were returning home from the hospital, the rickshaw was hit by an oncoming car. After a brief blackout, I woke up facedown on the road, my juda (hair bun) undone, patka (head covering) off, my arms bloody and my knees scraped. The rickshaw's tires had gone over my grandfather's legs, and my mom, who had been close to the scene of the accident, was screaming. Luckily, no one was seriously injured, save for minor scars, blood loss, and a concussion. The car driver, who had not been paying attention, paid off the rickshaw man, and we walked away with nothing. In India, it's difficult to sue or file a court case over such things when bribery and exchanging money on the streets is the law of the land. Shortly after the incident, my grandfather and his lover returned to Dhaka. It wasn't long before we heard the news that she'd passed away. As a child, I felt anger toward her due to the loyalty I had toward my grandmother; but as an adult, I only felt sadness for her passing and my grandfather.

Back in the day of my grandparents, arranged marriages were the custom. No one had a say in who they could marry. Even when my parents married by choice, they faced their own share of challenges, the most daunting of them all coming from my very own Bibi. She didn't approve of my Dad, who came from a different caste. Both of my grandfathers were responsible for negotiating the Treaty of Versailles that eventually led to the union of Gurvinder Singh and Harleen Kaur. But an alliance built on bad blood has a history of blowing up in people's faces as time passes. Just look at the Three-Fifths Compromise in the Constitution and how even the founders of America left out two-fifths of African Americans to not be considered as people, a system that legitimized the mistreatment of the minority population from Independence to the Civil War and the civil rights movement. Some may argue that the system still carries on today through mass incarceration and police brutality. My dad and grandmother were mortal enemies, more than any other son-in-law/mother-in-law relationship I have witnessed. My grandmother continuously objected to their match right up to their wedding day. After that, she refused to speak to my mom until I was born. This was not lost on my dad, and the animosity he expressed toward her was returned in kind at every opportunity.

From the moment we found out that Bibi was coming to live with us in Dover while Masi and her ex-husband were trying to resolve their differences in San Antonio, it was Battle Royale at the Singh household. Every single day, there was yelling, shouting, hitting, and crying—even when Bibi hadn't arrived yet. The same routine continued after Bibi came to stay, and I was scared to go to the living room whenever my Dad came home. Sonya, Bibi, and I stayed inside one of the two bedrooms in the apartment while we overheard my parents yelling outside. One night, Bibi had enough and she went outside to confront them. I don't remember how I got in between my parents, holding my dad back and saying, "Dad, I love you, I only love you; please stop." I was sitting on the floor besides my father and crying my eyes out while watching my mother and grandmother standing on the opposite side. It would seem that even my ten-year-old self knew that the person I had to get in front of was my dad. He was the one who could do the most damage with his loud voice or heavy hands, and my subconscious told me I had to calm him down. I don't think I could comprehend the curses coming out of my dad's mouth, but let's just say I have never heard anyone else speak in that way. Despite the number of uneducated individuals, homeless people, drug addicts, gangsters, and Scarface-like characters I would later meet in my life, none of them could top the ill words I heard that night.

A few decades later, I watched the movie *Saving Mr. Banks* and saw how the father in Mary Poppins's story always created a magical world for his children even when their life was spiraling out of control—and I thought about the stark contrast that had with my dad, who shared the impact of every bump life gave him with his family.

My mother came from a stable background. Her loving father, Bhupinder Singh, was an artsy type of man who loved literature and had published multiple books in India, none of them for the sake of royalties or wealth but to help the poor and spread knowledge, much to Bibi's dismay. He had also ventured off to Kuwait in the 1980s and 1990s prior to Saddam Hussein's invasion with his older brother, who was seeking the oil riches of the gulf. I don't think he ever cared for those riches, but Bibi certainly pushed him to become more financially stable rather than continue with his pursuit of becoming an educator, which generated a small salary. My mom's strong mother, Surjit Kaur, a.k.a. Bibi, was always practical, someone who often prepared for the worst. Her oldest daughter couldn't have been more different from her. Bibi told me once that when she was pregnant, she experienced a scary episode, which could have explained why Mom was always so scared. If there was ever a time to see the stark difference between mother and daughter, it was in the moment Bibi persuaded Mom not to leave America. Bibi was a strong, composed woman whose face seemed to have never known the look of panic; meanwhile, her oldest child was afraid of her own shadow.

Mom used to be a very confident young woman during university when she was in Chandigarh. She was even friends with Neetu Singh, the actress and wife of actor Rishi Kapoor. Mom was the person responsible for going to my paternal grandfather and pleading with him to approve of their marriage and speak to her parents, which was not the easiest thing to initiate in India in the 1980s. My father was also a very different man in college, as my mom would tell me. He was charming and sweet. He would ride his bicycle around, and he always just wanted to get together with my mom to grab some chai. But after marriage, everything changed. He became bitter and violent, controlling every aspect of her life. In the four years of their relationship prior to marriage, he had never raised his hand against Mom, but that soon changed. Growing up, I saw him slapping her in almost every fight, and he would also slap his children when we did something wrong. In India in the 1990s, no one frowned upon these events as it seemed normal to use corporal punishment or even beat your wife. I learned two decades later that this was in fact not the norm in well-educated Indian families.

Mom had to give up her PhD studies because Dad wasn't supportive—perhaps he was jealous. I wonder if that bitterness came as a result of the taunts he endured by Bibi. Mom always cited Dad as the reason why she became the person she was. I saw this even during the years when Dad was away in America. We had a loving home in India, but even as a young child, I saw Bibi as the strong matriarch of the household, never my mom. Mom was always very talkative, but her approach to relationships was more about pleasing others than asserting her needs. She was always more concerned about keeping the peace than standing her ground. This was not lost on me when I considered the relationship between her and my dad. In any argument or challenge, she resisted being involved in a long disagreement and instead opted for a meaningless peace. Their fights would be loud and sometimes physical, but nothing would change, and the same event would take place a few months or years later. When I was young, I always felt that if Mom had taken a stand, she could have changed her life and, as a result, our lives. If she had left my father when he crossed a line or demanded he go to therapy or a complete change of behavior, perhaps he would have thought twice before repeating his actions. I was so afraid of him growing up as was Sonya. I wanted to hate him for what he was doing to us but somehow I knew my father was not a bad person. I needed him around and I needed his approval even though I cannot forget what he did to mom. Whenever it was time for him to come home from work, we would turn off the TV and sit behind mom as if to hide ourselves from him. Mom would protect us if Dad went off like a time bomb at a moment's notice. The moment he saw us hiding behind mom, he would go off. It was an endless cycle of fear and resentment from all parties. We wished he would stop and I know he wished that his children wouldn't be so scared of him. He never knew how to express his emotions in a constructive manner and tell us that he wanted to be loved as well, not feared. But his actions continued and he never sought help to get better. Mental health has a stigma in Indian culture. "People will think I am crazy or mad, what will people say?" I wish that mindset was "what can I do to be better for my family?" And answered "whatever it takes." It's not fair to say my parents were always at odds with one another. There was romance, but it weakened as life's challenges kept getting stronger. Their love story peaked before marriage, and what I remember from childhood are events that scarred me from a young age.

During the years when Dad was in America, Sonya wasn't allowed admission into St. Theresa's Convent School because Irish Catholic Convent schools wanted to see a wholesome family unit for any child they allowed within their walls. I had gained admission only because Dad had gone in for the interview with a 102-degree fever, understanding how important his presence was in order for me to be considered. I wasn't a rich kid, but I was part of a group of such kids who used to have their servants show up at lunchtime with a mat and fresh lunch from home. It helped that my sports skills outweighed my being a Sardar (Sikh) kid in the middle of Hindu-dominant Haryana. Cricket and I were made for each other, at least when it came to batting and fielding. But it wouldn't be cricket that would eventually lead to my sports fame. One day, we saw one of our classmates gliding on the road with wheels on his shoes. He had recently joined the club at the roller skating rink in town, and I thought it was the coolest thing I had ever seen. The moment I got home, I begged my mother to let me join the club, which she did.

The first skates I owned consisted of a strap that attached wheels to my shoes. Meanwhile in the rink, there were boys with skates arranged in a single line that looked alien in the world of four-wheeled skates. Those kid's skates came from overseas; meanwhile, mine needed oiling before the wheels decided to move. But once I started skating, I felt like I was flying. The adrenaline rushed through me, and no matter how many times I would fall on my elbows and knees, I kept getting up to try harder. I never learned how to slow down on my skates, which became a problem when I would lose control and fall. I didn't have any pads either to save myself from the scars that would follow me for the rest of life. A month later, I joined the city competition for roller skating. When I unexpectedly won the gold and bronze medals, the coach's gaze fell on me. How the hell could this newbie with a poor excuse for skates win against the inliners fashioned with road wheels? The coach convinced my mom that I needed better equipment to compete at a higher level. After a few conversations with my dad, money came in from America for those shiny new skates, and along with it an influx of gold medals. My mom was very supportive—she woke up at 5 a.m. in the mornings to give me a lift on the back of a bicycle to my morning practices.

There were three races in competitive speed skating: the time trial, a.k.a. solo race with you against the clock; the rink race on either a wooden or marble surface; and the road race. I started training for the district competition, and my dad came home from America to witness it—I won all three events by lapping the competition in the six-to-nine age group. The 1997 state championship held in Panchkula, Haryana, had similar results—my family spread themselves out over the course of the road, with each member covering a hundred meters to cheer me on. There was a guy at the rink who had represented India in the previous Winter Olympics in 1994 and placed fifth in the world. He would show up to the building riding his metallic bike, and when he got on the rink, everyone would step away and watch. He wore fancy-looking tights along with his inline blades, which caught so much speed with little effort. I wanted to be better than that guy. I knew I lacked the grace in my races, but I took off every time with little regard for falling and hurting myself. I was determined from a young age to try harder than those around me, and every time the competition leveled up, so did I. My persistence and determination were built during this time—to never give up, to get back up even if I was bleeding all over my clothes to finish the race.

I remember the night of the state championship's first race as clearly as if I am there now. I was nine. The time trial race was at night, and the stadium lights shone on the white marble surface, making it gleam in shades of orange and yellow. Earlier in the day, I had realized that the speed of the marble surface would be much faster than the wooden rinks of Karnal that I was used to; in fact, the marble was the fastest surface I had ever skated on in my life. Before the competition, I had practiced in the rink to the song "I'm a Barbie girl." My English was good at the time, but I had no idea what the song was about as most of the music we listened to was in Hindi. The rhythm of the song was fast, the surface of the stadium was slick, and just weeks before, I had won three gold medals in the district championships. I was on top of the world. The moments in that lit-up stadium from that night have been the fondest memories of my childhood. My emotions were sky-high, not to mention that I would now have to perform in front of my dad, who was sitting right at the front with my mom. Dad had been away for about a year and a half, and this was his third time coming back to India since he had first left for America in 1995. I wanted to make my dad proud.

I launched myself forward the moment I heard the whistle go off. I flew on that rink, racing faster than I ever had. I felt light, and I was by myself as the crowd disappeared. My heart wasn't nervous; it was warm with the rush. Instead of leveraging the turns for breaks in my feet movement, I touched the ground and kept moving my arms and legs to go faster and faster. With every step and push on that slippery surface, I knew that I was going to win that gold no matter what. I was too consumed by the competition to worry about what was going to happen next in my life. I was somewhat of a big fish at St. Theresa's Convent School in Karnal, or so I liked to believe, but my life was about to take a dramatic turn, a turn that would occur at a faster speed than the turns of the race.

The next day, I was asked to follow a photographer from the *Chandigarh Tribune* for a photo shoot, with me as the state champion of Haryana. I did not know that that night in 1997 would be the last time I would stand on the stage to win the gold.

CHAPTER 3

IN THE JUBILATION of my state championship victory, I completely ignored the tea leaves. A year before that competition, Sonya, Mom, and I had gone to the US embassy in Delhi for our tourist visa interviews to join Dad in America. The pieces were set for our move, but only Mom's visa was approved. After that denial, I assumed we would remain in India, but Dad had other plans. On his next return to India, Dad reapplied for tourist visas for the three of us, and we made our way to Delhi to try again. Dad was determined to get us out of India so that we could have access to the opportunities that had been denied to him while he was growing up. India was a relatively new nation with a large population, and corruption was quite rampant. It was a developing country during that time, and my father didn't want us to be held back while the nation discovered its identity. It was clear within the first few minutes of the questioning that the interviewer was going to approve us, and the credit went to my father. His confidence and presence were comforting. Our visas were approved a month after the state championship, and I believed my dad could do anything.

Shortly after the state championship, preparations started for the national championship to be held in Pune in January 1998. Our Haryana team was camped in Faridabad, a city on the outskirts of New Delhi, with the athletes quartered in a Buddhist temple in makeshift beds. Training started at 5 a.m., and it continued all day long without any hope of proper nutrition or rest. Anytime you made a mistake, it came with a beating and scolding from the coach: "Mera bharat mahaan." You can always count on India to provide their athletes with absolutely nothing to help them succeed, not even funding or training, as evidenced by the movie *Dangal*. For my non-Indian readers, *Dangal* is about a national champion wrestler who has dreams of winning an international gold medal. However, he receives no support from his family or country. He does not win that international gold medal (go figure) and instead starts training his two young daughters to become wrestlers during the 1990s. The daughters go on to win gold medals in multiple international tournaments, starting with the Commonwealth Games in 2010, hosted by India.

After a month of nonstop "training" and "preparation," we were off to Pune, a two-day train ride away. It was winter time in Haryana, which is in Northern India, but summer in Pune in the south. When Dad suggested we take a domestic flight down to Pune from Delhi, our closest airport, the coach responded by saying, "Do you think your kid is special or something? If he wants to compete in the tournament, he will go with the rest of the team." I will never forget how our train would stop at night in some station in an unknown city, and people would board with the same ticket numbers as us because there wasn't a clear system to track sales and prevent ticket vendors from selling the same seat number twice. Our sleeping stations had to be shared at night with a random person. After two days of enduring the train system in India, we made it to Pune and I fell sick. The change of the seasons and lack of rest combined with improper nutrition had led to a poor immune system that couldn't handle all the beatings my body was taking. The national championship started two days later. The first race was the time trial competition. On our first day in Pune, we went to practice in the indoor stadium. Instead of marble, it was a cement-based rink. I had skated on wood and on marble but never on cement. In order to adapt to the new surface, my coach recommended switching into wheels that were more appropriate for the cement. They took out some bearings that made the wheels hold steady and never put the bearings back when they put my old wheels back on, a fact that wouldn't be discovered until after the competition was over.

I was a turbaned Sikh competing for the national championship and representing the state of Haryana, not Punjab. Sikhs only make up 2 percent of the population of India, and a majority of Sikhs live in Punjab. I was young and didn't yet think about the hate humans have for one another and their differences. Because of my background, the coaches were biased against me, and my parents said that that was the reason why they were not to be found during the competition to help or guide me. It was as if they had just disappeared. Their absence may also have been due to the fact that they lost interest in me once they found out that I would be leaving for America. To them, I did not have a future in competitive skating representing Haryana or India. I placed seventh in the time trial regardless, not knowing that that would be the last time I would place in any skating competition for the rest of my life. The road race was a total disaster; I couldn't breathe, and there were so many kids competing at the same time that I felt like I couldn't even see the track on which we were supposed to race on. The competition was over before it started, and I lost. All I had ever achieved before felt like it amounted to nothing. I was humiliated, embarrassed, angry, and inconsolable. The loss wouldn't have hurt so much if not for how it had happened. It wasn't fair. I would carry the pain of a lost career path and failed Olympic glory forever. I was so mad at everything that I ran away from my parents as we were walking around the stadiums after the competition. My dad caught me and beat the shit out of me—I blacked out and probably suffered a concussion. At the time, I thought I rightfully deserved it.

On our trip back to Delhi, we stopped by Bombay, traveling by train. In Bombay, now called Mumbai, we saw the biggest slums in all of Asia. Trains were so congested by an overflow of bodies that there was always a possibility of losing each other in the middle of the hustle and bustle. While in Bombay, Dad took us to a theme park—my very first theme park experience. It was freaking awesome. The roller coasters were scary but cool. I loved the speed we travelled at, even though it made my head hurt during the ride and afterward. Reflecting back on this as an adult, it's clear this had been my dad's way of making amends after his conscience kicked in.

The next day, we boarded the Jet Airways flight back to Delhi. Talk about an unforgettable experience. It was my first time in an airplane, and I thought it was so cool, orderly, and clean—even fancy, shall we say. Trust me, when you live in India, clean is a big deal because there is garbage basically everywhere: on the streets, buses, trains, and the ganda nala that runs by almost every street—a canal of sewage running out in the open. In comparison, the plane was like heaven as it flew into the clouds above everything else. I remember my ears hurting like hell and how the flight attendants gave us toffees to help with the pain from the air pressure. The coffee-flavored candy was quite hard to bite into, but they tasted expensive. The plane ride was over before it started—it only took us a few hours to travel back to Delhi on a plane in comparison to the two-day train ride from hell.

Back in Karnal, we were again in the middle of winter, so on went the sweaters and back into the suitcase went the shorts. Our departure for America was due in a few weeks, and it was now time to sell everything we owned before leaving India forever. Luckily, our furniture was in good condition. Our dining room set resembled that which was found on TV serials, the sofa was royal in appearance, and the bed sets were rich. One person came and took everything, even my bike. I cried so hard as I watched them load everything we ever owned into a truck. As it drove away, I ran after the truck with tears running down my face and pleaded that they at least leave my bike behind. In hindsight, it didn't matter because I would never ride my bike again, but tell that to a nine-year-old boy. Just like that, everything I had ever known was gone. We went to the man's place for dinner afterward and saw our furniture arranged in his brand new home. It looked nice, but it wasn't the same. It was no longer ours.

On February 18, 1998, we boarded our Lufthansa flight from Delhi to Frankfurt, then to New York City, and finally to Houston, Texas. The plane was a lot bigger than the lean Jet Airways domestic flight; it was like a giant in comparison with three rows of seats and a big middle row. I remember looking out the window and down on all the lights of the never-ending city of Delhi as we took off—they were so beautiful. This was my goodbye to the country of my birth.

I couldn't sleep at all on our flight. The entire experience was exciting and nerve-racking. The plane had an in-flight entertainment system with movies and a world map that showed the plane's path from Delhi to Germany. I was so distracted by the technology that I didn't stop to realize that the plane was my very own version of the *Mayflower*, carrying a new wave of immigrants to the promised land. When we arrived at Frankfurt, we were completely lost in the large airport and had to catch a ride on one of the airport shuttles to make it to our connecting flight. We had left Delhi at 3 a.m. and arrived at Frankfurt six hours later, with the sun shining bright overhead, and it was so bright on our flight to New York that I couldn't sleep. Finally, I succumbed to exhaustion and fell into a sleep that no one could wake me up from. When the flight landed and the passengers disembarked onto the tarmac, I was loaded onto a wheelchair and rolled out. The airport staff controlling the wheelchair hit a bump and I flew out facedown onto the tarmac, still not waking up. My mom, who was holding on to a sleeping Sonya, was pissed to say the least.

The domestic flight to Houston was quite bumpy with a lot of turbulence, but I remained fast asleep throughout. After landing, we made our way through the airport maze, which seemed to go on for quite a while. Finally, we reached immigration. There we were, about to enter the United Fucking States of America, in the great state of Texas. My mother was wearing a desi suit and holding the hands of her two small children, one of them with a patka. After a series of routine questions like "What's the purpose of your visit to the United States?" and "How long will you be staying?" we made it past without a hitch. Luckily, I don't think my mom responded to the officer by saying, "We plan to live here forever and never leave," which would have gone down very badly. We stepped outside the airport doors, and there we were—we had made it to America.

It was so clean. There was no sand or dirt or patchy grass or potholes in the roads. Right outside the airport exit, we saw smartly dressed men who turned out to be cops on bikes. They were wearing helmets that looked like the ones people wore during the skating championship. The buses were so fancy and high-tech compared to the Haryana Roadways buses, which were probably bore a closer resemblance to US buses in the 1980s. It was in these things that I started seeing what people meant when they said India was behind America by a few decades. Everything in America was so grand. But no one looked like me. I was used to what most people looked like in India, but this was new territory. The people around us were different shades of white and black. The people with similar skin tones to me had very different facial features. Everyone was really tall. I had never seen anyone who looked like the people in America before in my life. It would take me a few years to understand what everyone meant by the term *melting pot*, and I was a part of it now.

Masi's friend picked us up from the airport. I spent the next day sleeping like a baby in their beautiful house. It was such a nice place with a large backyard that even had a swing set! In India, we would always have to go to the park to ride on a swing, but in America, swings were in your own personal home. These people had every convenience we craved in India, including central air-conditioning. The next day, we boarded a Greyhound bus to San Antonio, and we were finally reunited with Bibi again, along with Masi and my two American cousins, Hardeep and Amanjot. Bibi had arrived in America a month before to help Masi out during the divorce. Masi was working full-time, and Bibi had to quickly adapt to her new life. She was already skilled with the ins and outs of her new home, including using the new technology of a microwave and oven that we had never seen before.

Hardeep was the same age as Sonya. He had a bowl-shaped haircut, the type popular with parents in the 1990s. Hardeep and Amanjot were darker toned than the rest of the family, their shade and hair a courtesy of their father. Amanjot was two years older, with pigtails that would be fashionable among the young girls in our family for the next few years, as well as a Kajol-style unibrow. The first meeting between the cousins was awkward. Our language and cultural barriers were on full display. My Indian English accent wouldn't go away for at least three to four more years. It was also strange to us when Hardeep and Amanjot would leave for three days at a time to spend time with their father since divorce and joint custody weren't common in Indian society. We stayed with Masi for a few weeks until Dad came over from his restaurant job in Austin to announce that we were moving to the great state of New Jersey where he had found employment at a gas station pumping gas for Mr. Kohli. Mr. Kohli was a full-turbaned, bearded sardar who was true to his religion and who owned a bunch of Texaco gas stations and convenience stores throughout New Jersey. It was a three-day Greyhound bus ride from San Antonio, Texas, to Swedesboro, New Jersey, which "helped" us see more of America in three days than we would see in the next ten years. Besides running through the bus station in the middle of the night in Nashville to arriving on a rainy morning in Cherry Hill, it was an unmemorable journey.

New Jersey might as well have been the Ellis Island for Indians coming to America, a rite of passage, the sign that you had arrived in the New World. Mr. Kohli picked us up in his red Ford F-150 pickup truck and dropped us off in Vineland, New Jersey, at an apartment with four men who were meant to be our roommates and that had no furniture, an awful smell, and garbage all over the floor. I cried like a toddler whose milk bottle had been stolen when I realized that we had left everything behind in India for this shit. But the kindness of strangers came to surprise us all when Raj Sangha, another employee of Mr. Kohli's, took us to his apartment and let us stay with him and his wife for a while until we could afford a place of our own.

Over the next two years, we lived in Swedesboro, Sickersville, and Vineland, New Jersey, where I attended three different schools. In the second school where I started fifth grade, I was placed in a special education class because I wasn't picking up American English as fast as my teachers preferred. A month later when we moved to Vineland and I attended Landis Middle School, I made honor roll every marking period. Sonya, who had only been four years old when we first arrived, started prekindergarten and kindergarten during these years, and so she wasn't experiencing the same growing pains as her older brother, whose legal name, Arjun, was giving him problems in school. I was looked upon like an alien by the middle school kids who had never seen a young Sikh boy before. I was nine years old, and I had never had a haircut in my life. My hair was braided and wrapped together in the middle of my head and covered with a patka. When we finally moved to Dover a year later, we had moved around four school districts in three years. Allowing a newly arrived immigrant child to adapt or make friends just wasn't my family's top priority. The primary focus for our family was surviving and living like nomads, a pattern that would continue for quite some time. It was unclear to me why we had ever left our lives in India to come to this place, and it would take me another ten years to figure that out.

CHAPTER 4

FOUR YEARS AFTER our arrival in America in 1998, just when our lives looked to be improving, the rug was pulled out from under our feet. We had settled down in Dover for a few years and moved from Towne Point Apartments, located in the rougher part of the city, to the Baytree neighborhood. Dad had purchased a new minivan with automatic sliding doors, and along with the apartment, our life was starting to resemble what we had left behind in India. Masi had bought a townhome in the same neighborhood, and I could easily skate over to see Bibi or play with Hardeep, which I did almost every day while Dad was at work. But then came the knock on the door in July 2002, and everything turned upside down. A few months after the events of that July afternoon and Mom's decision to leave, Dad and Masi decided it would be best that we all live together. I guess it was an effort to show that their marriage was legitimate or to save money, or both. It was a good thing this took place after the worse had already happened. They decided to split all the bills evenly—in return, Dad would live in the basement while Masi, Bibi, Hardeep, Amanjot, Sonya, and I would live upstairs in a three-bedroom, three-level townhome. What could go wrong?

It must be against human psychology to adapt to a new person living in the same vicinity, especially people who truly dislike one another. Add in the fact there was only one full bathroom to shower in for seven people, and you can imagine the fallout. The importance of a bathroom can't be overstated, as I would realize far later in life—similar wars are fought every day all across this country of ours. During this time, there were two women living in the house who truly disliked my father and who blamed him for what had happened. Masi was upset that Dad had let the immigration officer into her bedroom and closet to investigate when he should have kept a cover on parts of their story. To Masi, everything that had happened was Dad's fault, and she had gotten caught up in this mess for no reason. After the episode in San Antonio that had left Masi and my cousins on the street, her ex-husband had given up joint custody. She went on her own separate way and opted only for child support without fighting for a share of his assets from the divorce, displayed a strength that almost seemed mean-spirited to me, a trait that I saw consistently during our time together. At least that was how it appeared to a child who had no idea of the other adult interactions that might have happened in the background.

Despite the tension between Dad and Bibi, it was nice for me to have the opportunity to live with Bibi once again and not feel completely alone. Bibi was the only consistent parental figure I was accustomed to having around. I still hadn't processed Mom's sudden departure, and the tense atmosphere in the house gave me little breathing room to heal. The only person who understood my pain was Bibi as I was afraid to ask Masi or Dad about what would happen next. Even though we could talk to Mom on the phone, we could not conduct our conversations freely around the other two adults. Both Dad and Masi had resorted to making harsh comments about each other behind the other's back, often passing blame or insults. I wanted to confide in Mom and tell her about what was going on, but with the telephone located in the living room where either Dad or Masi was always around, it was hard to share my true feelings in fear of retaliation. But when only Bibi was present, we could speak our hearts out. One night, Bibi called Mom and sat at the top of the stairs with Sonya and me by her side, crying about what had happened to her children. Bibi, who never cried or showed any sign of weakness, revealed a moment of vulnerability, in which we all found some comfort.

That year, in the fall of 2002, school began in the narrow hallways of Dover High School, a building that was a small earthquake away from falling apart. I was about to start freshman year at Dover High as a taller, thinner adolescent boy. As if the turban on my head with a large bun wasn't enough, puberty was making things so much worse. I was assigned to a few honors courses, the most advanced being Algebra 2, followed by Biology, and then World History with Ms. Beck. I will never forget the *Harry Potter and the Sorcerer's Stone* poster Ms. Beck had on her door when I first walked into class, and my instant feeling that I was going to like her. I'd always loved history ever since I had Mr. Cash as my sixth-grade history teacher. In history classes, I would teleport to far-flung destinations based on the topic we discussed. When Mr. Cash taught, I felt myself present in Ancient Mesopotamia, Ancient Egypt, Ancient Rome, and Ancient Greece. I always had a good memory, but I wasn't just memorizing dates of events but also imagining myself present during these time periods: how it would have felt like to be living in Gaul when Julius Caesar conquered the territory and sold men who fought against him into slavery, or to become gladiators to provide entertainment for the Romans, or to be in Western Africa in a tribal battle and be captured by an adversary only to be sold off to a slaver and shipped to America. I remember almost every detail of every history class I had ever taken since Mr. Cash, though I don't recall any topics about India. Meanwhile, biology was something else entirely. I entertained the possibility of pursuing medicine as my career so I could eventually become a wealthy doctor who would get my mom back to the country and give money to my dad so he would be happier and nicer—at least that's what was going on in my thirteen-year-old mind.

On the other hand, gym class was painful. My early athletic ability had disappeared over the past four years of junk food and no sort of competitive sports for me to participate in, minus gym. There was a reason for my hunched shoulders and poor posture. At some point during eight grade as I entered the early stages of puberty, my chest started growing, similar to breasts. I was suffering from gynecomastia, better known as man boobs. I wasn't overweight, but there were many origin theories that Mom and Dad came up with. Maybe it was because Dad overfed me eggs—he used to make me eat four to five eggs a day. He always believed that the nutrition we got with our food in America was far superior to what he had grown up with in India, so our bodies should reflect that. Even though the excessive eating of "good, nutritious food" eventually became unhealthy, he was adamant that I should be grateful for what was sitting in front of me on my plate. I hoped it was just a passing phase that would go away as I grew older, but it remained for the next two years, making gym class a nightmare, especially when all the boys lined up with their shirts off for a physical. Fuck my life, I thought. My problems didn't stop there. My eyesight started giving out in my freshmen year, but I didn't want to add glasses to my already super attractive looks or tell Dad that I was becoming deficient in multiple ways. I didn't want to add more problems to the list because it seemed the adults had enough on their plates. It started becoming a real issue when I couldn't see the PowerPoint slides on the screen at the front of the class or actively participate because I couldn't read the sorcery my biology teacher, Mr. Mo, was writing on the board. I started pinching my eyes, which made it easier for me to see temporarily, and so I made do with my situation without being completely helpless. I didn't tell anyone I was going blind and kept up the facade for as long as I could.

This was also the first time I saw seniors kissing and hugging in the hallways. Was this allowed? To my surprise, it was, and no one said anything about it. My hormones were starting to go nuts, and naturally I always wished I was the guy kissing the girl and holding her close—but instead, I was Osama's son. The Patriots winning their first Super Bowl with some no-name sixth-rounder wasn't the only big thing that had happened in the last few months. The September 11 attacks the year before had changed the world for everyone, but mine was completely torn. The bullying, the side glances in the hallways, and the slick comments in passing started instantly. My seventh grade teachers would stop me in the hallway to make sure I was all right even as I entered eighth grade. It was nice of them to care and I felt their compassion, but they couldn't sit with me at lunch or look out for me in the boys' locker room. I was alone with no friends.

Happily, there was a large skating rink in Dover. During that time, Derek Parra had just won two medals in the Salt Lake City Winter Olympics. I read in the newspaper that he lived and trained in Dover at the local rink, and flashbacks and a glimmer of hope came back to me—maybe my own dreams weren't completely gone. Whenever it was possible, I would ask Dad or Masi to take me to the rink. On the rink, all my pain would vanish. I felt free as I glided past everyone, often being yelled at by the skating referees to slow down. I had kept up my speed over the past four years. There used to be a skating team in Dover, but they had to shut down due to financial problems. The closest one was in Philadelphia, but no one could drive me there to train or participate in competitions while working at their jobs.

Dad worked in the Dover Mall at USA Blues, a store that carried Sean Jean, Timberland, and whatever other version of Yeezy's there was twenty years ago. It was the longest job he had maintained since coming to America, going on his fourth year. Most of my clothes came from Dad's store or things he would pick up for me at JCPenney, Macy's, or elsewhere in the mall during a sale. He would get the extra-large size of some polo shirt for himself and get me the same clothes in medium. I would be dressed as either a young Slim Shady or a middle-aged man. Due to his pending immigration status, Dad could not get a job back in the banking sector working normal hours, so he had to settle for what was available through the local Indian connection network. USA Blues employees worked six days a week, from ten to nine, with a required presence on the weekends. Dad formed friendships with the managers at the mall movie theater, and in return for deals at USA Blues, he would get them to let Sonya and me into the movies for free. Call it a poor man's form of babysitting or parenting techniques by using a combination of Bollywood and Hollywood. No wonder we turned out so dramatic. Once, Hardeep, Sonya, and I were able to see *The Lord of the Rings: The*

Two Towers, and we were so blown away that we kept going back to see that same movie another four to five times. We weren't familiar with the story, but nonetheless, all three of us were enchanted by Tolkien. A little imagination and fantasy were a logical attraction for us when no one wanted to be anywhere near the reality we were living in.

Sometime in the winter, things in Masi's townhouse entered Cold War territory. I couldn't tell who were the Americans and who were the Soviets. The wartime analogy was appropriate as President Bush had just given Saddam Hussein forty-eight hours to leave Iraq or prepare for the worst. Dad wasn't talking to Masi or Bibi. He used me as a messenger for whatever he wanted to convey to them, and they did the same from the other side. Bibi had no choice but to talk to him in the mornings during breakfast or at night when he would come home. To be fair, he was paying for half the groceries, so at the very least I thought he should get some food and a few words in before dessert.

Meanwhile, I was developing a close friendship with Hardeep. Hardeep was a good, light-hearted boy who somehow looked up to me. However, Bibi wasn't very nice to him and always treated him harshly and unfairly for reasons I was not aware of. Was it because he was darker skinned? Or did he remind her of his father? We had already bonded prior to the events that had forced our joint-living arrangement, playing in the streets of Baytree, riding bikes, or playing basketball. When Hardeep, Amanjot, and Sonya tried to skate in the streets, it was a pitiful sight. Instead, Hardeep would just join me on his bike while I skated past everyone, going into a fast run while I jumped from the road to the grass to avoid falling from a sudden change of surface. We shared common interests in video games and sports, especially in our passion for the Philadelphia Eagles. We were brothers.

Meanwhile, Sonya was building her own friendship with Amanjot, one that I didn't envy too much. It was boys against girls. Amanjot had an attitude during those early years, and a lot of her issues stemmed from her separation from her father. The traumatic events of what her father had done to them in San Antonio caused her panic attacks. I was too young to understand or be of any comfort to her. We didn't share common interests and kept our distance. Besides the fact that all of us were now being raised by single parents and Bibi, our lives were still different. I started having regular nightmares of the government busting through the doors to imprison us. I also began sleepwalking. Once while sleepwalking, I walked out of the house in the middle of the night and stood in the snow. I thought the door to the house was locked, so I sat outside the front door, screaming and freezing for hours before I came to my senses and went back inside with purple hands and feet.

One weekend, while I was sitting downstairs with Dad, I just cracked. I couldn't stop crying. What was happening to my life? Mom was gone, I had no friends in school, and coming back home scared me. Minus Goku and the Power Rangers, who else did I have? Sure, I had just discovered the masterpiece written by J. K. Rowling after watching the first Harry Potter movie, but that magic wasn't entering 500 Schooner Way's basement. No one was happy in that house, and after the school year ended, Dad, Sonya, and I made our move to Salisbury, Maryland. We were leaving the city and the only family we had in the country with nothing.

CHAPTER 5

SALISBURY WAS DIFFERENT from Dover in a lot of ways. It felt like I had crossed the Mason–Dixon line. Salisbury was a smaller town with a population that was very white in comparison to Dover. The minority population was small and poor, filled with working people who would easily fit the roles of the Viola Davis movie *The Help*. Dad continued to work in retail, now at USA Wireless selling cell phones provided by Cellular One, soon to be bought out by Cingular Wireless and then AT&T, in the Centre at Salisbury, a.k.a. the Salisbury Mall. I started school at Parkside High, which was across the street from our new apartment, conveniently called Parkwood Apartments. There was another apartment building called Parkside Apartments down the road . . . you get the gist. I was going into my sophomore year knowing absolutely no one.

Growing up, we never had many Indian friends, nor did my Dad. We always felt like outcasts among the rest of the community. After all, how many financially unstable Indian families lived in the US? Most of the community was well-off financially, and even the individuals who had come here in ship containers or by jumping the border had since established multimillion dollar business empires. Dad had been in the US since 1995, and it was already 2003, and we were still going paycheck to paycheck with no hopes of becoming legal or wealthy anytime soon. In Salisbury, there was Tishcon, an Indian-founded vitamin supplier company that employed almost every Indian in the city. Salisbury had a big desi population, and it even had a mandir. Most of the population, who were fairly successful, were from the state of Gujarat. Then there was the Punjabi population: the young guys in the mall, working in the kiosks or the cell phone stores. The image of a Punjabi was the same all across the country: laid-back and a failure even in the New World. We were the drunkards and the fighters, not the businessmen or the highly educated. Basically, we were perceived as the Black people of India or the Irish in America in the early nineteenth and twentieth centuries. The stereotype was created for a reason and then reinforced over many generations. This was our image, and I believed it was up to us to change it. And it would take time . . . a little longer than I wish it had taken.

I tried to assimilate into my new zone of desi influences. It was the time of AIM (AOL Instant Messenger), Yahoo! Messenger, and MSN Messenger, and boy, was I unprepared. As a young, adolescent Sikh boy trying to fit into a new crowd, I thought I'd say something to be cool. I said something mean about a girl, and it was fucked up—something along the lines of her being hairy or ugly. Damn, what an asshole I was. It backfired, and my message spread like wildfire. The next thing anyone knew, the entire city knew I'd said it. I won't forget my fuckup to this day, and every time I see her name pop up on social media, it is a strong reminder of how wrong I was to have said something like that to a person who did not deserve it. I guess I had done the same thing that those other desi kids had did to me: make someone a scapegoat to take the attention away from yourself and to appear cool and part of the group. At the core, I just wanted to belong to something, but instead I alienated myself within weeks of arriving in my new city.

Luckily, Dad had been in Salisbury a little bit before we had gotten there and had made some connections, including a couple called Rajesh and Michelle. Rajesh, an Indian man, had married Michelle, an American, after coming to the US. Michelle was a very religious Black woman from the South who really wanted to help my sister and I in the new city. She would often pick Sonya and me up and bring us over to their house while Dad was at work. Rajesh was a top-notch chef and a professor at UMES, the University of Maryland Eastern Shore. They had a son, Avinash, or Avi, who was an aspiring skater and who became our friend. We went to the Salisbury skating rink once, and he was blown away by how fast I could skate. The rink used to do races, and I would repeatedly lap the competition. Once, a guy who was a few years older than me challenged me to a race, and I beat him. Avi told me about Apolo Ohno, the recent Olympic record–shattering American speed skater, and we practiced skating on the street by his house or we raced with him on a bike and me on skates—and I still beat him. My skills won me some fans, but my skating talent was fading away without proper instruction or a structured pursuit of my dreams.

Despite my friendship with Avi, alas, the Indian taboo of the color of your skin couldn't be overcome even in America, and it affected our relationship with Michelle. In India, lighter skin was seen as better; and the darker you were, the less attractive you were perceived to be or whatever other nonsense that is part of my culture and my people. I took part in this belief myself—I remember buying Fair and Handsome creams in my late teenage years even though I was already fair skinned. What the actual fuck was I thinking? It's so easy for stereotypes and racism to become a part of you. Prejudice and ignorance, that's what was in our heads and what many of us continue to think and believe. Dad or other grown-ups would make comments about Rajesh and Michelle's interracial marriage, especially how Rajesh had married a Black woman. I never heard them use derogatory words to describe her, but I could tell what they meant from their tone. Subconsciously, those comments influenced how I thought about other human beings because of the color of their skin.

Michelle was too kind and too proper, and we didn't appreciate her as much as we should have, especially when it came to her sharing her beliefs with us. When you get stuck in a room with a serious believer of Christ who is trying to convert you, you could care less about God, especially when your mother is half a world away. I lost all faith in God during this time. Even though I learned Punjabi when we moved to the US, I went from praying daily from multiple Sikh holy books when we lived in New Jersey to no longer believing in God by the time I got to Salisbury. Can you blame me? So, I thought whatever Michelle was saying was bullshit, and I wished she would just stop. She tried everything to help us integrate into the new city, even taking us to the Hindu temple and making me the speaker for a play the temple was doing to celebrate India's independence from Great Britain. For the play, I narrated the list of British atrocities performed on Indians during colonial rule from the 1800s. The actor playing the freedom fighter screamed "Vande Mataram," the national song of Indian independence which literally means "I bow to the mother, motherland. I bow to the motherland," while the British soldier whipped him. The song was banned by the British as it was used as a rallying cry for the Indian freedom fighters. That was the height of my popularity and participation in the Indian community of Salisbury. I never took part in any other program or function. Then, Dad said something to Rajesh Uncle that pissed him off, and we broke off our relationship with Michelle as well. Dad would go on to repeat this habit of saying something to piss another person off many more times throughout our time in America, thus continuing to limit our relationships with the outside world.

And so our world was limited to watching the latest Bollywood movies in order to stay in touch with our people and culture and our perceptions of how relationships were built. In addition to the well-choreographed dance numbers in exotic locations, most of these Bollywood movies were love stories about couples navigating through a complex web of relationships among family and friends to finally reach one another. For example, the hero would be a light-hearted partier who belonged to a rich family and who fell in love with a simple girl from a different background. There would be multiple obstacles in his way to get her, including getting her conservative father to approve of their match in a fight against the other guy in the love triangle who had an old friendship with the father. Or the movie would be about a large extended family living together (father, mother, grandmother, grandfather, brothers, and wives all in the same house) and how their dynamic would change when money and other issues arose. How many Americans could imagine watching a movie that promoted the idea that a family should all live together under one roof? It's hard enough for a husband and wife to be constantly on the same page; now imagine adding multiple other people who are maintaining their own relationships into the mix. I thought it was just stupid, especially from my experience living in Masi's townhouse in Dover; I believed everyone needed their space. But the person who would be against these concepts in the movie would be considered the villain, portrayed by the most evil-looking comic book character you could imagine. Clearly, Indian people valued this picture of an ideal family. Meanwhile, my American peers had a very different idea of how families stay happy and have healthy relationships, and it didn't look like a Bollywood movie of family members constantly being on top of one other without any space to themselves. Thus I experienced the constant clash of American/Western culture versus the Bollywood representation of Indian culture and values. This inner war would continue to define me for a long time to come, highlighting the differences between an individualistic and a collective society.

Meanwhile, my sophomore year of high school was off to an interesting start with puberty in full gear—and there were all these pretty girls with golden hair around me. In the midst of all the shit that was going on, I knew one thing for sure: I really liked girls. They were so pretty. That's what I needed in my life to get my mind off the misery of my situation—women. The concept of getting married made sense to me now. It all started in ninth grade, when I walked into high school and saw the older kids around me kissing and holding hands. There would be a make out session going on beside your locker, and in front of you, kids were walking to class holding hands. I had never seen that in middle school. We were growing up, and our hormones were going nuts. It was like someone had given us a drug that turned on all our senses, which were mostly directed toward the opposite sex.

Ashley was a girl in my history class who was always nice to me, so of course I was attracted to her. She was thin and blond and wore braces. I didn't have the guts to talk to her and tell her I liked her. I was terrified, so I thought, why not write her a note? My plan was after she'd read it, I would ignore her like the plague, and she would just come to me if she liked me back. That's how my series of failed attempts to woo women started. I mean, give this pimple-faced, patka-wearing, patchy-facial-haired, skinny little dude with man boobs a real shot to get a girlfriend! Well, let's just say I was going to fail at getting girls for quite some time.

I also wanted to start playing sports again, so I figured since I loved the Philadelphia Eagles so much, why not try out for football? Yeah, that was a solid idea. The kids around me had grown up watching and playing the game, and I couldn't even get the helmet on right thanks to the bun of hair on the top of my head. It certainly didn't help that my eyesight was getting even worse at this point. I had avoided getting glasses or contacts for the past two years by cheating on my eye exams and pinching my eyes to get a clearer view. But nonetheless, I was going to try out for football! And tried I did, taking multiple hits repeatedly from boys twice my size. Every time our helmets banged together, it hurt. Once, a kid tackled me so hard while trying to catch a punt that my helmet flew off and I blacked out. Coach Polk came up to me and said, "Welcome to football." The Will Smith movie *Concussion* hadn't come out yet, and the dangers of concussions weren't a big concern during this time. So I kept this up all throughout sophomore year, regardless of how bad I was at the game. It gave me a sense of belonging, even though we would say the Lord's prayer at the end of every practice or at the beginning of every game. I joined in even though I wasn't Christian. Then again, getting everyone to say the traditional Sikh prayer "Akem kar, satnam karta purak, nir poh, nir wher, akal murakh . . ." wasn't going to happen. Once, I was sitting on the bench and a cheerleader came up to me. She asked me about my hair and if she could touch it. Off went the fireworks. Somebody call an ambulance, because I was having a heart attack. A girl talking to me? Shut the front door. If this had happened some other time, I would have been offended at the request, but at that moment I was just happy a girl wanted to touch me at all.

I daydreamed about her and me ending up together, like in those

Bollywood movies. I hadn't yet discovered porn or sex, so having sex wasn't coming fully to mind. I am sure many of my young peers around me had the same visions going on in their heads. It turned out that even Harry Potter was going through the same struggles of teenage-hood. The fifth Harry Potter book, *Harry Potter and the Order of the Phoenix*, was set to release at this time, and young Harry was experiencing a lot of the same issues I was. J. K. Rowling must have known how old I was because Harry was always the same age as me when the books came out. His feelings for Cho Chang and the anger he was starting to feel toward the adults in his life felt familiar. The only difference was that once Harry learned who he really was, he was no longer invisible or seen as a freak. Meanwhile, I wasn't anything special to the population of Salisbury on the Eastern Shore of Maryland, minus the extremely strange braided bun of hair on the top of my head. Most of my classmates had known each other from middle school or elementary school—their families had known each other and they had grown up together. I, on the other hand, had only known everyone for a few months.

I met Carolyn Williams in Mr. Dinges's advanced chemistry class. She wouldn't know it for the next few years, but she would become the Hermione to my Harry and the Sam to my Frodo. She was a sharp young woman with dirty-blond hair, and she had attitude and wit. I would often butt into the conversations she was having with her friend Anisa in chemistry class to attempt to build a relationship with them or get answers to tough chemistry questions. There were a lot of questions I was clueless on, so my interruptions were quite consistent. Many varieties of the word *annoyed* would be used when Carolyn thought of me for a long time to come. It's fair to say at this point that we were anything but friends. I was just the annoying new kid in her chemistry class.

My relationship with my father was also getting complicated during these days. I barely ever saw him. After so many years, it was evident that he would never have an opportunity to work in a white-collar career, and that frustration consumed him. He was working with people who were high school dropouts and who did not share his intellect, which left him unfulfilled. Most of his coworkers were also undocumented immigrants, just like him. Dad had had a ten-year business visa when he first came to America, but if you don't return back to India every six months after entering the United States on that visa, it is no longer valid, which is how he lost his legal status. Some of his coworkers had found their way to America by jumping the border or hiding in ship containers, but ultimately it didn't matter how anyone entered the country—everyone was equally undocumented and in the same boat. His coworkers were of Punjabi descent, either from Pakistan or from India. Some of them had claimed asylum to become legal while others had gotten married, and everyone was slowly finding a way to gain their freedom except us. Faced with this, Dad started taking an interest in his health instead, focusing on the things he could change rather than the things he couldn't control. He changed his diet and went to the gym every morning before work, and he pushed Sonya and me to do the same, telling us to go to the YMCA to become physically healthy.

In order to make life bearable or distract ourselves from reality, we continued to rely heavily on movies. Cell phones weren't widely available at the time, and we didn't have a home phone either, so we had no contact with our family in Dover, barely seeing them all year. It was always up to Dad to decide when an occasion to visit would take place, usually without any prior notice to Sonya or me. Dad's cell phone was the only way we could communicate with anyone. Meanwhile, my conversations with Mom were controlled by Dad—he would decide when we could speak to her, and he would always be close by, listening in. I guess he wanted to know if we were complaining about him. At this point, it seemed like everyone had formed the opinion that it was all Dad's fault that everything had gone wrong, and he didn't want his children to also feel that way. However, in his attempts to keep those thoughts under wraps, he made us feel suffocated. Either way, our conversations with Mom were mostly a repeat of her expressing her guilt for leaving us, and unwittingly, I was becoming numb to her words.

After working his eleven-hour shift, Dad would come home, and we would just sit in the living room and watch the latest Bollywood film. God, they made a lot of movies, and most of them were either about the same shit over and over again, or they were a copy of a Hollywood movie. In Indian culture, children aren't really encouraged to be very creative. Parents want their kids to be more practical and to focus on things that will make them successful in the future, such as being a doctor or an engineer. Playing is for losers or "lafange lokh." The cultural belief is that if you want to be something in your life, you will study; and real success is achieved through education and only in the fields of medicine, business, and engineering. This trend was highlighted by the great Bollywood movie *3 Idiots*. Dad wasn't a fan of the movie because it touched on exactly those issues—the standards that Indian parents of the 1990s follow to this day like it's some religious practice that we must all abide by. Did these parents ever stop to think that learning about other things like history can help us to learn from the past and to not repeat the same cycle of mistakes from our ancestors? Or that art can be therapeutic and priceless? Why do the rich collect pieces of art? Because you can't put a price on creativity or beauty. It's more valuable than all the books that teach you how to solve "a squared plus b squared equals c squared," which can make you feel like a square afterward. I'm not saying it's wrong to like math and to want to study those things because they have indeed contributed to the advancement of humanity, but not everyone is built for that. Let me play, let me draw, let me run, let me fly—just let me be me. That was my outlook on life.

CHAPTER 6

IN 2004, I started working at McDonald's in the Salisbury Mall on the weekends. I looked at the job as a good way to get me out of the house on the weekends, where I could be productive rather than just sitting at home watching movies or playing video games all day. I had a young Gujarati manager who was very ambitious in his McDonald's career, with a full Gujju team and me. Literally the only person who wasn't Indian at this Mickey D's in the Centre at Salisbury was the guy who cooked the meats and then swept the floors. We would later find out that the Gujarati manager became greedy at some point, creating a job for a fake employee whose checks would go to him. The things people will do to deceive others and get more money! The attraction and greed of doing nothing more than what you're already doing but getting paid extra for it is strong. For the rest of my life starting from that moment at McDonald's, I knew how hard I would have to work to honorably move up the food chain and become successful. Thus began my journey on a capitalist path. I learned that the harder you work, the more you make.

In the middle of the school year, we moved to government housing or HUD, which was a lot cheaper than Parkwood Apartments. It was the hood of Salisbury, many times referred to as Little Islamabad because the people who lived there were mostly Pakistani. I was no longer in the Parkside High district and would have needed someone to drop me off and pick me up after school. My other option was to transfer schools to Wi-Hi, a school that represented the neighborhood it served—poor minorities. Though I was one of those minorities, I didn't want to be a part of that group. Maybe I thought I was too good for them, too smart to go to that school, or just too scared of getting jumped or killed in that place. Though I had survived Dover High School a year earlier, which had also served difficult neighborhoods, I had become accustomed to Parkside High School and really liked the environment there. I remembered the bullying I had been subjected to in the hallways of Dover High, and I was finally feeling safe at Parkside.

In geometry class at Parkside High, I would meet the first angel to come into my life, Alex. Alex was my first real friend since we moved to America six years ago. She was quiet, sweet, and super smart, and she always wore nice sweaters. Prior to joining Parkside as a freshman, she had been homeschooled, so she didn't know anyone else, either. She was thin with red hair and pretty features; she could have been a Weasley in the Harry Potter series. We became friends and formed a little group with Sharde and Shenay in the back corner of Ms. Kyle's geometry class. Sharde and Shenay were part of a school exchange program from Wi-Hi and only attended geometry class at Parkside. Our friendship did not go further than the hour of geometry we spent together, but it was nice to feel comfortable with them. Together, we were the outcasts, and I finally had someone to sit with during lunchtime. When we moved to the new neighborhood in Salisbury, Alex got her older brother, Brian, to start driving me home from school so I wouldn't have to leave Parkside. Thus began our true friendship.

Around this time, a lot of negative influences were starting to creep up around me. On my fifteenth birthday, Dad invited some people over to celebrate, including a bunch of older guys he worked with who started passing me beers. The taste and the smell were god-awful. Years later, after I passed through my binge-drinking phase of Natty Light, Keystone, and Bud Light and discovered craft beer, I realized why my first beer had tasted so bad. During this time, I could have easily pursued the option of drinking myself out of my senses and taken advantage of the fact that I had access to people who could buy alcohol for me, but my sense of righteousness wouldn't allow for that. In the back of my mind, I knew this wasn't my path. Dad used to drink quite often, but I had always been taught that alcohol is bad and that I shouldn't do it. I often heard stories of how Bibi beat Mamaji, her son, with a chappal (slipper) several times when he showed up home drunk. I certainly didn't want to get beaten by a chappal and especially not by Bibi. She was a daunting personality—I saw the fear in Dad's face whenever he was in her presence—and she had never even raised her hand against me. Even though she was currently living apart from us in Dover, I didn't want to disappoint her.

I wish I could have stayed in Salisbury a little while longer, but that summer we moved again, this time to Silver Spring, Maryland, in search of a higher-paying job for Dad who was working for another Indian business owner in a USA Blues–type shop. He was doing his best to earn more income to send money back to Mom in India every month. But there was always going to be a limit on how much he could earn doing mindless babysitting of one retail store after another. He didn't earn enough and didn't have the knowledge and connections to open his own business, which would require proper documentation to implement, so he kept his head down and continued doing what he could. All those years he spent in the banking sector learning finance and enabling others to become financially successful had resulted in him never being able to do the same for himself. We left Salisbury suddenly, at a time when cell phones weren't a thing. Alex and I never exchanged home phone numbers, and we didn't have emails or Myspace, let alone Facebook or Instagram, to keep in touch. After my family left, there was no way to stay in touch with my first friend in America.

Silver Spring was different from Dover or Salisbury. It was an actual city with a large downtown area, metro access, and crowded streets. The guy my Dad was going to work for was a fully bearded, fully turbaned Sardar who owned a clothing store. With the larger paycheck came a more expensive city, but this one was very diverse. There were actually sardar boys in my school! Holy crap, I thought I was the only one (a line made famous by the comedian Russell Peters). The first day at lunch, I ran into a guy with a turban that was different from mine. I was still wearing my patka, and this dude was wearing a full turban in a different way than Dad had used to wear his. His was not pointy in the front but equally shaped on both sides, and flatter, just wrapped around his head. Sukhbir was a devout follower of the faith. He was older, wiser, and so cool. No wonder the Sikh girl in our lunch group who also wore a turban like his was totally in love with him, even though she never admitted it.

Soon after arriving in physics class in my new school, we were paired into twos for a group experiment that involved racing cars, and I was put together with a girl named Sarah Brown. She didn't think it was weird that I wore a turban, which was a first for me. She came up to me and said, "I am going to beat you," in an almost flirty way—and there it was, my first true crush.

Sarah Brown was different. She knew I had a thing for her, but instead of avoiding me, she made me a part of her group. Sarah, Jason, Katie, and I became friends. Jason was Sarah's ex-boyfriend who had been in love with her since tenth grade (and who was still in love with her). Katie, Sarah's friend from childhood, was a little, round, pale young woman and a goth. Once when we were hanging out, Jason picked us up in his car and we all went ice skating in a big rink. Though it was on a different surface, I was back in my element, gliding on the ice. And there was Sarah with her black, wavy hair and sharp features—maybe a little Native American with a mix of some European ancestry. I was falling hard for her. Thanks to Sarah, I learned to enjoy the life I was living. She was a lively personality who just wanted to enjoy herself, and it didn't matter to her that people called her names. She was like Emma Watson's character from the movie *The Perks of Being a Wallflower*, and I was definitely similar to the freaky outcast. Sarah always had a boyfriend, and the man in question that year was Doug, a tall, broad boy with hair just like Justin Bieber in the early days.

Over the course of junior year, I got a job at another McDonald's down the intersection of Randolph Road and Colesville Road. During this time, Bibi came to live with us as we needed her more than Masi and our cousins. With me starting work after school, and no money to get a babysitter, someone needed to stay at home to look after Sonya, who had just turned eleven. My relationship with Sonya was like any sibling relationship during the early years, where we didn't have much in common minus the bad hand we had both been dealt in life. She was in elementary school while I was attending my third high school in three years, and I wasn't as kind to her as I wish I could have been. She was also without her mother, and instead of coming to her defense or being there for her during these times, I would often call her chubby or pick on her with my cousins Hardeep and Amanjot in the rare occasions when we would all see each other.

During this time, I started taking the bus to Downtown Silver Spring to get my driver's permit. The night classes were held in a basement of a building. It was the cheapest driver's education program I could find, so I couldn't complain about the location even if my commute to Silver Spring was scary. I had never been alone at night in a city like Silver Spring, and I had to navigate the dark streets from my class to the bus station, especially with my poor eyesight. This made my driving practice lessons with Dad in the passenger seat even harder as I still hadn't told him that I was practically blind. I was already scared of driving our big minivan in a metro area like Silver Spring, and add to that the fear of messing up and crashing the car, along with the fear I felt just being in Dad's presence. It was a disaster waiting to happen. Luckily, I finished my hours and practice with him without any incident.

We were a long way off from affording to buy another car for me, so I had to improvise with what was available. From Monday through Friday, the city bus went all the way down the road to the McDonald's I worked at, but it only traveled half of the route on weekends. On Saturdays and Sundays, I would get off halfway and skate to work the rest of the way. The route I had to take was hilly, with the road getting very steep at certain points. The skates would pick up a lot of speed, and I had very little room to balance and navigate the road. God forbid there was a bump in the sidewalk or the road, because if I fell going that fast on skates with no helmet, that would have been a serious injury waiting to happen. The fact that I couldn't see clearly past a few feet in front of me also made skating on the road the worst idea imaginable. But I had no choice. I understood that if I wanted a car, I had to work. Skating at night was even scarier, especially when it snowed and there was a possibility of black ice on the road. I don't know how many times I could have died while doing that trip—but luckily, I didn't. I lived and overcame the darkest moments of that year. My ability to skate had never earned me an Olympic gold medal, but at least it had given me survival skills, such as never giving up and finding creative ways to overcome any challenge that came my way.

My grades would be the worst of my life during this time. Bs and Cs that had never been seen on my report card would become a constant, especially in trigonometry, physics, and Spanish 4. For all the desi kids out there, imagine your parents seeing that you got a C grade—all they see is that C, and not the reasons you got the C. I was ill-prepared to handle the curriculum of Paint Branch High School compared to the schools I had attended in the towns of Dover and Salisbury. They were much further ahead in their learning and at a level I could not catch up to. I had been in three different school districts with different curriculums in three years, and it had finally caught up with me. I couldn't adapt.

But I continued on with life. On February 14, 2005, I kissed Sarah Brown. Sure, it happened during a game of spin the bottle at Jason's house, but it still counted! And it was incredible, the feeling of your first kiss with your first big crush. Your lips on her soft lips. Talk about goose bumps and the feeling of being on top of the world. But that was the closest thing we ever came to having a romantic relationship. At prom, Jason decided to send Sarah flowers at the pre-prom dinner at the Cheesecake Factory instead of coming to prom with of the rest of us. Doug, Sarah's boyfriend at the time, was pissed, and the two of them spent the entire night fighting at the Lord Baltimore hotel. Apart from the drama, prom was a great experience—we had a limo and everything. Of course, I was the only one in our group without a date and I spent the night solo, admiring the red balloons everywhere and the grandness of the venue.

Usher's "You Got It Bad" filled the room, and there were some emotions in the air. The girl I had a thing for was with her boyfriend, and there I was, alone. After prom ended, we stayed up until 3 a.m. in the morning playing games. It marked a transition from our time as kids in high school to adults, a sign of what life would be like in a few years' time. College was only a year away, and the school year was coming to an end. And this would come with yet another move—watch out Salisbury, we were coming back.

CHAPTER 7

THE DAY WE got back to Salisbury, I drove my new Toyota Corolla to Alex's house behind Parkside High School. It was a duplex property, and I wasn't sure if she still lived there, but I went there anyway and knocked on the door—and there she was. She was so happy to see me, and we shared a giant bear hug. We caught up, and I told her that I was back. We had both gotten cell phones since my departure and now had the ability to communicate before the school year started.

During the summer vacation before starting my senior year at Parkside High School, I finally confessed to my dad that my eyesight was weak. Now that I had been working for the past year, I decided it was only right to go for an eye exam. Living silently with my handicap for the past three years had always made me feel less guilty because I didn't want to put another financial burden on my father. My eyesight was negative 2.5, which I am sure had deteriorated quite a bit from when I first noticed the problem in my freshmen year. I was fitted for glasses but I opted for contact lenses to address the issue. Meanwhile, I got my old job back at the McDonald's at the Centre at Salisbury, as well as another job working the water massage units at a different kiosk in the mall. The last but not least of my multiple jobs was selling cell phones for USA Wireless, a job I would continue for the next eight years of my life. A job that would get me through college without a single penny of student loan debt, and a job that would also help me pay for my car and our house mortgage.

There was another thing brewing in my heart during this time—the desire to cut my hair and fit in with everyone else. I was tired of being the Sikh boy with the turban and the facial hair, which connected from my mustache to my beard. I wanted to cut my hair, style it, and shave. I wanted to have girlfriends and be popular. Sure, I knew it was important to stand out rather than be like everyone else, but tell that to the kid who just wants to kiss someone, to have friends, and to belong (think Disney's Hercules trying to fit in among the mortal world with his godlike strength, though no godlike strength for me). One night, I took a walk around the neighborhood and called my mom on my new cell phone. Finally, I told her about all those years of being picked on and bullied, outcast and alone, and how much I wanted to not stand out anymore. Having a cell phone of my own and the ability to speak freely with her without Dad eavesdropping on our conversations had reignited our relationship. I had never spoken so honestly with my mom like I did that night. It felt liberating to finally share my feelings with her. So Mom told Dad what we discussed, and the next day, Dad said, "Go to the Hair Cuttery down the mall and do it if that's what you want." In fact, Dad himself had been a clean-shaven man since his second trip to America back in 1996, but I had still been expected to continue our religious beliefs. Though he had given me the green light, he didn't approve of me cutting my hair and made his disappointment felt verbally and visually. I believed if only he had known how alone I'd felt, he wouldn't have acted so mean-spiritedly toward me.

All of a sudden, I transformed. I was going to the gym every day that summer. My hair was cut, my facial hair was shaved, and my eyes worked with the help of my contacts. I was good looking. The girls who wouldn't look twice at me before started talking about me behind my back in school. Girls now had crushes on me through to senior year. Finally, this was what it felt like to have others desire me and want me. Even so, I knew who my real friend was throughout all of this. Alex didn't see me for my pretty face; she had seen my soul all along. Nonetheless, I loved my newfound fame and attention, especially when the teacher would announce my name during roll call and people would pause to look and say, "Wait, that's Arjun???" The boy with the bun on his head had come back with gelled hair, American Eagle polo shirts, and a muscular build. Gone were the years of timid man boob–filled anxiety, and gone were the man boobs, which had been surgically removed in the summer. My body had transformed to that of an athlete, later to be demonstrated by my vanity when I used my cell phone to send a girl a picture of my abs, a display that would be used against me for more than a decade after the incident. And gone was the fear of not being wanted and being alone. My group of friends expanded, and I became confident in who I was. I might even have had five or six casual girlfriends throughout the year. Alex and I started doing monthly dinners at Applebee's, and our table just kept growing with new friends. I quit my other jobs and worked at the Cingular franchise, USA Wireless, every day after school and on the weekends. Cingular would later merge with AT&T and become AT&T wireless. I had money, as well as a Toyota Corolla that my McDonald's job from Silver Spring had provided for. I had independence, and I loved every moment of it.

As senior year at Parkside High School flew by, so were the plethora of FAFSA forms, college essays, and recommendation letters. The race to apply for colleges was about to start, and the entire year was dedicated to that next step. We were made aware over and over again that "your life is about to start, and you should go to college if you really want to be something in the world." I avoided thinking about college for as long as I could. Despite my successes in school, I was still an undocumented immigrant who was ineligible to file for FAFSA or get into college and pay in-state tuition or receive any scholarships or grants. I was fucked. Although my GPA had come back with a vengeance, along with all sorts of confidence, and even though I had been admitted to the National Honor Society and had five AP courses that year, my college dreams were not going to happen because of my status. So I continued to ignore that part of my future and enjoyed my new life and the joys it brought. Once, I went to the immigration office to figure out what my status was and how I could change it. It was just pending. Our case had been pending for years, and I didn't know what to do to change that. It wasn't just the inefficiency of the government; we had known from the beginning that our case was fucked up and that the office probably just hadn't updated the status.

As a possible solution, I tried to enlist in the Marine Corps and the Navy. It would have been nice to belong to and be part of a greater calling even if it meant being shipped off to a war zone in Iraq or Afghanistan. Dad was willing to sign off on the papers as I was still seventeen at the time. He didn't really know what to say when I started meeting with the Marine Corps recruiter; there weren't many better options available to me anyway. During the Marine Corps process, issues came up with my sleepwalking, and I needed a psych evaluation that I couldn't afford because I had no health care. When I went to the Navy recruiter, he was at a loss for words when I told him I wasn't a US citizen but that I wanted to serve so I could become one and help pay for college. Unfortunately, a future in the military wasn't meant to be. During this time, George Bush was also trying to pass the Dream Act, providing a path to citizenship for kids brought to the US as children by their parents, which gave me some hope.

I continued to gather recommendations and write college essays that I never planned to send off. Even if I got into college, I knew that Dad or I wouldn't be able to afford out-of-state tuition. So what was the point of applying? Or worrying about something that was out of my control? Strangely, during this time, I encountered some mysterious coincidences. I passed several AP exams and scored the highest on the biology exam and was awarded nineteen total college credit hours. When I received the science award for graduating seniors, I was presented with the award by the same Navy recruiter whom I had left speechless during the interview process. I then received my first detention in senior year for being late to class for the third time, even though I was driving to school and no longer taking the bus. As I sat down to fill out a pamphlet explaining why

I'd fucked up, the teacher who was monitoring detention started talking about college. He told me that he was still paying off his student loans but that he didn't regret it one bit. It so happened that the detention date was also the deadline for fall admissions at Salisbury University for Fall 2006. That day, I ran out after detention and drove to the Salisbury University admissions building before the office closed at 5 p.m. and handed in my completed application that I hadn't mailed out. A week later, I got my acceptance letter. It was the only college I had applied to. Dad said, "I will pay the admission fee, and that's my gift to you. You can figure out how to pay for the tuition." Tuition . . . holy shit. It was $3,400 a semester, and that didn't include textbooks. Even though I lived at home, Dad was making around two thousand dollars a month with no savings, with rent to pay for and two kids to raise. I had to stop spending all my paychecks on clothes from American Eagle, Hollister, or Aéropostale (seriously, what the fuck was I thinking back then? I was basically a model for the preps). I had to start thinking about how I was going to pay for college while making six dollars an hour.

That summer at the new student orientation, everyone else was there with their parents, brothers and sisters, and grandparents. I was sitting by myself, just like I had been the day I received the President's Award—everyone else's parents were sitting in the audience, but no one was there to support me. In moments like this, it became all too painful that Mom wasn't around and that Dad couldn't afford to take time off work to show up to his son's award ceremonies, football games, or his new student orientation for college. The orientation was overwhelming, with a moving opening remarks session by Dr. Mullins, a chubby guy with glasses and a white beard, about five-foot-ten, with parted black hair. Although it was hard sitting there and hearing him say, "Look to your right and left, and applaud the people who are proud of you for accomplishing this great feat of starting your journey at Salisbury University," I applauded like everyone else, even though I didn't have those people with me. Regardless, I was loud and confident that day of orientation—until they asked me to put a major down on my file. I hadn't even thought about what I would study in college; I was just so happy to be here. I put down English as my major and tried to make friends and introduce myself to everyone in our group sessions.

And then came the first real sign that there was a God and that he had listened to my prayers. When I attended the financial aid session, I learned that Sallie Mae (a financial aid service) offered a program for student loans that would break up tuition payments into four zero-interest payments with a fifty-dollar fee that had to paid within four months after the start of the semester. There it was, the solution of how I would pay for college: using the pay-as-you-go strategy. Over the past summer, Masi had offered to cosign a student loan application through Bank of America at a rate of 17.99 percent. She mentioned during the phone conversation that she would always help me, but not my Dad, and I understood why. I appreciated her effort, but a 17.99 percent interest rate starting from day one was no match for a government-subsidized loan of between 4 to 5 percent with no accruing interest. With the help of the Sallie Mae program, it became possible for me to get my financial goals on track.

I opened my first bank account at SECU because older clients who came into Cingular always told me that credit unions were the best. I listened to everything they had to say because I wanted to learn from successful people and grow. After my eighteenth birthday, I waltzed alone into the branch to open my first account. I asked if there was a way not to bounce checks, and the banker recommended an automatic line of credit attached to my checking account to prevent those fees. I was approved for an unsecured line of credit of five hundred dollars. I knew funds were going to be sparse, and I didn't want to pay unnecessary fees. I also got a credit card account with a five-hundred-dollar limit. Starting August 1, college tuition payments would be due for the fall session. That summer, I worked every day in the 118th Street Cingular store, making $1,600 a month with commission. I worked from ten to eight every day and from eleven to six on Sundays. I would be paid in cash because I didn't have a work permit, and I would give all that money to Dad to pay for my car and help out with home expenses as we had bought a ranch house at the height of the market in 2006.

I made it to my first day of college and stupidly picked an 8 a.m.

class that I would not show up to on time for all semester, not even once. Blame me for not getting up on time or getting a parking permit, but the fact was I was low on funds. I was unaware of the attendance policy in that class, and even though the course was for people who hadn't taken AP US History, AP European History, or World History, and I knew everything our Egyptian lecturer was trying to teach us, my A was dropped to a C grade because I was thirty minutes late to a forty-five minute class every Monday, Wednesday, and Friday. In fact, the only reason I showed up to the class at all was because of Caprice Kefauver. My god, she was beautiful, with the most beautiful eyes. Unfortunately, I could not work my senior year magic on her, and our love story never took off. I had never been to a party at this point in my life, minus that one weekend night during high school when Alex, Eddie, Mahgoub, and I went to a hotel room in Ocean City and got drunk off Smirnoff Ice. And considering that I still lived at home, partying would be rather difficult with my militaristic Dad on the watch. But I did take advantage of my newfound freedom in college to start driving to Dover to visit my family with Sonya. I tried to reestablish our lost relationship since high school graduation by being more present and taking an active part in my family. I missed Bibi, and I missed hanging out with Hardeep, who was growing into a popular high school athlete. However, our meetups would be short-lived, and they rarely came to Salisbury to return the favor. Masi wasn't a fan of driving, and it probably wasn't a pleasant experience for her to be around Dad, but it still left a sour taste in my mouth and Sonya's. We always tried harder to be a part of their lives; in a way, we wished our lives were more like theirs.

By the time October came around, my line of credit's balance was maxed out and I had to work more hours to pay it off or consider selling my own cell phone to make ends meet for the December tuition payment. When customers came in to upgrade their phones after eighteen months, I would often convince them to leave their old phones behind. Facebook Marketplace wasn't around at the time, and many of these people didn't have a need for the old tech. I would then sell these phones on the side to earn some cash that could help buy a newer edition of an economics textbook instead of buying an older version with out-dated page numbers that made doing homework assignments impossible. College was a scam in that way, and using the "current" version of a book compared to the edition one year older was the highlight of their crony capitalism. Imagine making six dollars an hour after the end of summer and paying $850 a month just for tuition, not including buying new textbooks, some of which cost more than a hundred dollars. At this point, I discovered the art of hustling and Half.com, a sister website of eBay where you could buy old college books for cheap. I would get cheap books and, at the end of the semester, try and sell them for more than I had bought them for. A true capitalist.

It was hard as shit to adapt to college life. You were responsible for picking your classes and schedule and making your own free time in between to do whatever you needed to do. You were responsible for figuring out your own life. No one was going to hold your hand and relax their expectations because you were struggling and juggling so many things at once. I lacked that discipline my first year of college, and it got worse in my second semester when I decided to pledge a fraternity. Or rather, the fraternity thought I was pledging and simply brought me along. I didn't even know what fraternities were at the time or that you had to pay to be a part of one; I wouldn't find that out until after I was initiated and realized I had to pay dues. Fuck, I didn't want to sign up for that. I barely had money to eat as it was! I just wanted to party and make friends, plus meet some girls. The only social interactions I was having at this time was with my high school peer, Carolyn, via AIM conversations in the evenings while I was at the Cingular store.

I went to my first fraternity party thanks to Shahid Afridi, a snake and a sketchy motherfucker who worked at the Verizon kiosk across from our store. He was a fellow brownie, but from Pakistan, American-raised. He was my competition and from the enemy country! But the main reason I didn't like him was because he was often a dick to me. One day, I noticed he was being uncharacteristically nice to me. The pledge process had started, and they clearly needed to recruit more people to be part of their fraternity. He invited me to a Sigma Pi party and picked me up in his car. Beside me in the back seat was the person who would become my new best friend, Vincent Johnson. Vincent could have been Justin Timberlake's doppelganger. He essentially had the same features as Justin, minus the gelled tips and Britney Spears as his girlfriend. He was from Carroll County, Maryland, and he had a large personality and a loud voice to go along with it. My first college party was wild. There were girls and music and red solo cups everywhere. We smoked weed out of a beer can with a girl both Vincent and I were hitting on, Amy Moon. Neither one of us got the girl that night, but we did become friends, and our friendship continues to this day.

I got the bid to be part of Sigma Pi, and thus began two nights a week of pledging activities, which gave me a reason to be on campus outside of classes and staying out late instead of going home after work. I met Carlo, Kanye, Frank, and Shane in my pledge class. We did dumb shit while pledging, from being blindfolded and kidnapped to an empty field, to being targets of a water balloon fight, to going around campus and getting our bodies signed by girls and getting their numbers. But I had fun. It gave me a group to be part of—or at least that was what I thought when we were pledging. It turned out that after pledging ended, everyone would return to their own cliques and do their own thing. I started going to socials where fraternity and sororities would cohost parties so I could meet girls. I had gone from being popular in high school to being a nobody in the bigger pond of college. I was still a virgin, and even though my high school girlfriend had been totally down for sex, I was scared shitless. I didn't want to get anyone pregnant or get a sexually transmitted disease or any of the other scary things adults showed you in sex-ed to stop you from having sex.

After a few months of constant AIM messaging, Carolyn invited me to a New Year's Eve party she was throwing at her friend Dan's house. There were a grand total of five people at the party, including myself. As the night continued, from our initial awkward in-person meetup after a largely online relationship to cheap alcohol being consumed, people started pairing up for the big moment at midnight. The odds weren't in my favor, and I was drunk and about to pass out on the ground as

Carolyn and Dan made out on the couch, until Carolyn threw up and particles of vomit splashed on me. That moment could have gone in two very opposite ways: either we would never talk to each other again or we would never stop talking. In a weird way, it brought us closer and started a tradition of always spending New Year's together.

At the end of my freshmen year, my GPA stood at a whopping 2.6 when I needed to have a 3.5 cumulative average in order to stay in the honors program. I switched my major to political science because I had some credit hours carrying over from my AP exams. I also thought: Why not become an immigration lawyer and inspire change? In my first political science class, my professor, who was also the chair of the department, made his opinions on the current administration very clear. We discussed the war in Iraq from a completely different perspective compared to what I had learned in high school and through Fox News. There was no rhyme or reason for us to be in Iraq when we were already involved in a bigger conflict in Afghanistan. But it made perfect sense to increase American influence in the Middle East now that we had the world's sympathy after 9/11; at least that's what I think Dick Cheney must have been thinking. It was yet another example of present-day imperialism that had evolved from colonial rule. I realized that there must be another motive for the Bush administration to open two fronts in the region. Both Afghanistan and Iraq share a border with Iran, so why not suffocate the enemy regime that refuses to kneel? We failed when the Shah of Iran was overthrown, so why not install two puppet governments in Afghanistan and Iraq to put regional pressure on them? The weapons of mass destruction were never found because they didn't exist, and in our attempt to bring "democracy" to Iraq and Afghanistan, we contributed to increasing the national deficit, sacrificing American lives, and bringing about two decades of war only to leave the region more unstable than when the British first pulled out after World War II.

I continued to learn of other such examples with South America during the Reagan years and destabilization tactics in Nicaragua to beat the communists. It happened in Nicaragua, Korea, Vietnam, Iran, Afghanistan, and Iraq, and we only have South Korea to consider a victory of this tactic the US government has employed since World War II. In an effort to protect American interests abroad or to defeat the Soviets in Afghanistan, we created a generation of other problems by fighting the people the CIA had trained in the first place. In a global world where gang members serving time in LA prisons were deported back to Venezuela or other Latin American countries, they utilized their superior tactics and strategies learned in the United States to destabilize existing government systems that didn't have the capability to fight back. This in turn started a migration pattern of people escaping the war the US had started on their streets to move to the US itself, only to be demonized again as illegal immigrants. It all started making sense once I learned the origin of these conflicts. If we could stop these bad policies from being implemented in the first place, then we would have more resources to fix existing problems. But we had to admit that there was a problem in the first place, and that we were contributing to it.

After my freshmen year, I never signed up for an 8 a.m. class again. I was better with time management, and I took time away from the fraternity as much as I could without being kicked out in order to pay for college and get good grades. Every penny I made was going to college, and I worked all the time to pay for it. I had to make working a priority over girls and partying if I wanted to succeed, and so I did. If I attended fraternity events, I left halfway. I stopped going to socials, and I focused on my health and fitness. I got to know a lot of people through college, but although it was nice to not be an outsider, I was always away at work, and it was difficult for me to form the close bonds that I sorely wanted with people. Most of my friends lived in dorms and partied together, ate together, and studied together; meanwhile, I was at the AT&T store until 9 p.m. every night. I spent most nights by myself at home, watching a movie on the computer, chatting with Carolyn, or doing my homework. As much as I wanted to be part of the larger social group in college, I was stuck in my situation and I had no choice. I had to sacrifice my relationships in order to continue my studies, or I could just party and fail. At the very least, my friendship with Carolyn was growing, and I would often ask her to read over my papers prior to clicking submit. She was a much better writer than me, plus her focus on Latin American studies was somewhat similar to the poly science courses I was taking.

In my sophomore year of college, my credit score received a boost from my credit limits increasing, thanks to good payment history. The New Year's Eve to usher in 2008 was a completely different story: Alex, Carolyn, Kanye, Hardeep, Ray, and I were among others at a house party thrown in a beautiful family house belonging to one of our high school peers. Ray was completely head over heels for Alex and hated her ex-boyfriend, Aaron, who had spent the majority of the past year pursuing her. After many drinks, Ray finally crawled over and asked Alex if he could kiss her, and then he proceeded to throw up on the floor, making his way to the bathroom and ending up naked in the family room. Carolyn and I spent time with my fifteen-year-old cousin Hardeep, whom I had decided to bring to the party to give him his first alcohol experience. We watched in awe as Kanye, decked in a cape and top hat, asked Hardeep to do shots with him. Safe to say Hardeep had a fun New Year's, exclaiming on his way home that it had been the best night of his life. In a drunken state of emotions, Carolyn and I shared a New Year's kiss and a long hug, declaring how we would always be there for each other. Safe to say she was no longer annoyed by my presence. Just a week before New Year's Eve, I had met Carolyn's parents for the first time, and we attended a midnight Christmas service at Trinity Church in downtown Salisbury together. I was becoming a part of her family, and it made feel so happy. New Year's 2008 was the cherry on top of a great year—my best New Year's to date.

After winter break, it was time for my best friends to leave town and return to their respective colleges. Life continued as it had before. I discovered the website RateMyProfessor.com before the start of my spring semester and started making excel sheets to best plan for upcoming courses, along with the finances required per semester. I became obsessed with planning my class schedules based on when certain courses were offered and which professors taught them. It was a good feeling to break down college into four-month sequences rather than four years, and it made the cost feel less massive as well. I became extra studious that semester, refusing to go out and cutting down on my drinking ans socializing outside the mandated fraternity events or meetings. I had a long way to go before getting off probation from the honors program, and my cumulative GPA was finally over 3.0 as of the last semester, so I couldn't afford another mistake. My only form of socializing was catching up with Carolyn on Google Chat, as AIM was now compatible with Gmail. She was always helpful when I found myself stuck in both my political science essays or in life. I felt like she was becoming my guardian, and whenever I doubted myself or found myself lost, she was there as my guiding light.

When the final book of the Harry Potter series, *Harry Potter and the Deathly Hallows*, came out in the summer after the spring semester, Carolyn and I went to Barnes and Noble for the midnight release. At the bookstore, we ran into so many people we knew from high school, and it was one of my best memories of being young and free as a recently turned adult at eighteen years old. During the event, an Indian girl started talking to me. I liked the attention. We exchanged phone numbers and began chatting on the phone. One day, her dad called me, asking, "Why are you calling my daughter?" Talk about scary and unnecessary, and thus ended the short-lived love story between us before it could even start. It turned out she had been lying the whole time and had not made it clear that she was also seeing someone else. The story ended with little tears and kept me away from Indian girls for a long time.

But my connection to India was kept intact through Bollywood, my father, and whenever we got a chance to speak to Mom. I hadn't cried once in the six years after Mom left. Our weekly phone conversations were still monitored by Dad, who listened in at a close distance, the conversation screened with a similar effect to how the Chinese must censor their citizens. My mother was still a tape recorder stuck on the same ten seconds on repeat, saying over and over again, "I never should have left; I can't believe I left you two." Those two lines became her reality the moment she got on that plane alone at JFK. I was getting annoyed by the repetition and the lack of action to fix the problem.

But the truth was that nothing could be done to change the situation since Dad couldn't become legal in the United States and the Dream Act had failed to pass in Congress multiple times. We had to keep living in limbo, hoping that someone would eventually change this narrative.

Growing up, Dad always told me, "Teenage years are the golden years. It's in those years that you become who you will become, so don't mess that time up." In my golden years, I never once learned how to express the emotions I'd felt after Mom left. If I were to cry, who would I cry to? After all those years of being outcast, I was finally accepted . . . but how could I tell the people around me that according to official US government paperwork, I still wasn't an American? When they asked me where my mom was, I lied over and over and over again. When people asked me what my dad did, I lied again. I got caught up with trying to build an image of my life without accepting the emotions that had led to who I was. I was going through a phase where I would return home, go to my room, and start a movie, which I would watch all night until 2 or 3 a.m. in the morning. Sonya would be in her own room, which was decorated beautifully in comparison to mine. My sister had turned into a sweet girl in front of my eyes, far removed from her childhood arrogance, and I hadn't noticed it. Meanwhile, I never snapped out of living like we would have to leave the country at any moment, so I never bothered to decorate or personalize my space, whether it was my room at the ranch house in Salisbury or my future office or apartment after school. These are the small traits you carry with you after experiencing trauma, an ongoing battle in your subconscious that other people might easily miss.

One night I watched an Indian movie called *U, me aur hum*, where the female lead has Alzheimer's, which causes her to forget about her husband, her kids—everyone. I could probably have figured out the rest of the story without having to read the synopsis, but whatever the case, when I got to the part where her husband tried to get her to remember her loved ones again, something broke in me that night. Just a month earlier, Mom's visa application to return to the US had been rejected for the second time since she had been exiled to India. I cried my eyes out in my bed for what felt like hours. It was the first time I realized how I felt about my mother leaving and not having seen her in over six years. I was tired of being strong; I needed the nurturing only my mother could provide. I missed my mom so much.

CHAPTER 8

IN THE FALL semester of my junior year, my life was about to change. Everyone was coming back over the Bay Bridge to Salisbury after the long summer. There was a social planned the weekend before the start of the new semester, with the theme "dress like someone you're not." I was not the creative type, so I just wore a pink shirt, a color I often didn't wear. My friend Dustin Kruger, who picked me up, was wearing a shirt that said TKE (Tau Kappa Epsilon), the name of a rival fraternity. It was more original than mine, so I couldn't judge him. Dustin was another strange character—tall with German attributes, from his name to his looks. I had Sonya cover for me at home like I always did whenever I would be out late.

Five minutes after arriving at the house and talking in the kitchen, Nicole Adams walked in. She was wearing a pink dress, looking like a character from a 1960s American movie, complete with a headband and all. Nicole was from Anne Arundel county in Maryland and had been a head cheerleader during high school. She was tall and blond with elf-like features (something my family would say about her quite a few times). I walked up to her the moment I saw her, as if a force of gravity had taken over. We spent the whole night talking along with her friend, Michael Parlin, who would later become my other best friend, and Michael's girlfriend, Christy Baker. We just connected, which was hard to believe when you consider our backgrounds. How could a rich (well, she looked rich), gorgeous white girl have anything in common with a poor, brown boy? I guess people have more in common than just their net worth.

I was crazy about Nicole. I couldn't stop thinking about her, and I was not going to stop until we were together. I asked her for her number, and she invited me to her birthday party a few weeks later, this time with the theme of black and white. I couldn't wait until then to meet her again, so I asked her out before the birthday party. Our date turned into a weird three-person event at Uno's Pizzeria where she brought her sorority sister, Jackie. Thank god Jackie didn't come with us to the movie afterward. I tried to hold Nicole's hand after the movie, but she was not feeling it. I wasn't going to give up so soon. A week later, Michael, Christy, and I went to her birthday party together. It turned out there was another guy she liked at the party, but I wasn't shy about making my feelings known. Whoever that guy was, he didn't do anything to strengthen his case with Nicole that night, and I got into the only fight I'd ever been in when one of Nicole's uninvited party guests called her a whore. I pushed him, and we fought for a solid two minutes before we were on the ground. His friend caught me from behind and had me in a choke hold while I kicked his friend, and Mike Parlin tried to fight the guy to get him off me. It was probably comical to watch, but the cops showed up, and the party ended. Hero Arjun would get a call from Nicole the next morning, but it was not to share her feelings of admiration for my heroism but rather to scold me for starting a fight at her party. I told her that a guy had called her a whore and that I had pushed him and told him to shut up, which started the fight. There was a sudden change of tone. As much as some women say they don't like guys fighting over them, in this case, it seemed Nicole would have disagreed.

I suggested we redo her birthday with Mike and Christy in September. We blindfolded her on the drive to Ocean City and surprised her with an ice cream cake from Giant and a balloon. We played arcade games, and

I watched in awe as the two women crushed Dance Dance Revolution. Finally, we went to the beach, where she ran into the water, and I went in after her. She came back with her arms raised to give me a hug. "This is the best birthday of my life," she said. I lost my balance as the waves came crashing in and I fell backward into the sand and water. It was a cool, beautiful September night, with a breeze that smelled like seawater. It couldn't have been more romantic. I tried to kiss her, but she turned away. I hadn't totally won her over yet.

A few days later, Nicole invited me to her place to watch a movie. Her room was in the basement of the Alpha Sigma Tau (AST) house on Virginia Avenue. We were watching *August Rush* when she came up to hug and cuddle with me. She fell asleep during the movie, and the credits rolled with her lying still in my arms. I didn't move the entire night, afraid to wake her. The truth was I also didn't want this moment to end. When she woke up in the morning, I looked at her and she looked at me. "Why are you still here?" she said. Then, we kissed and kissed. This kiss was different than any other kiss I had ever had before. I was almost in disbelief as our lips touched. I wasn't just attracted to her because she was beautiful; I was feeling something I had never felt before. My heart was beating so fast, and I couldn't muster the power to lift myself away from her. I was falling in love.

Nicole started coming over to my place, sneaking into our ranch house even when my dad was around. There were loud crickets in the basement of her sorority house, and she couldn't sleep well there. We didn't have sex the first few nights; we just hugged and fell asleep together. We didn't cross that line until we were ready. A few weeks of this continued, and one night, the time was finally right. Ever since that night at the beach, I had been mesmerized by her. I had never slept next to a girl before. Holding her close to me made me feel warm and safe. Kissing her sent chills down my spine. I knew I was with a kind human being. All I wanted to do was make her feel loved and be loved. There wasn't anyone else I wanted to be with in that moment. Later that same night, I was at another house party for a social, and she came over. When Mike Parlin asked, "Are you guys together now?" I said, "We are going to be together for a while." She looked at me and said, "Oh yeah?" All I wanted to do was hold her hand, look into her eyes, and kiss her with every ounce of love in me. We started dating as boyfriend and girlfriend after that night. It was my very first real relationship.

CHAPTER 9

A GREAT MANY things were happening in the background while I was in college. The majority of my family was in Punjab, India—Patiala to be exact, a city six hours north of New Delhi that had become home to my extended family after my great-grandparents migrated from Rawalpindi during the partition. India became an independent country in 1947, and with that independence agreement, Pakistan was born as a concession to the Muslim population of India to have a country of their own. The idea was that if you were a Hindu or Sikh, you could still choose to remain in Pakistan; and vice versa if you were a Muslim in India. But that didn't go as planned. According to the Indian perspective, Muslims started executing Hindus and Sikhs in Pakistan, and their actions were returned in kind by the Sikhs and Hindus in India. An estimated two million people died during the great peace of 1947, including my grandfather's family members on my dad's side.

The story got even more diabolical when family betrayed family in the midst of their world collapsing around them. My great-grandfather had two other brothers, one older and one younger. The elder brother was retired from the army, where he had served British India, and the younger was still on active duty, stationed in Jalandhar, India. My family members were landowners in Rawalpindi, soon to be Pakistan. When the partition happened, they left everything behind and made their way to India so quickly that my grandfather, eighteen at the time, was given a coat by a bystander at the Lahore station. His exact words seventy years later were: "I couldn't believe my life had come to this—that I had to wear someone else's coat." He didn't say those words out of arrogance but to acknowledge the violent change of circumstances. When my family arrived in Patiala, they lived in a refugee camp. My great-grandmother passed away during this time, and when my great-grandfather filed a claim in Delhi for the loss of life and land, he realized his younger brother had declared the entire family dead during the partition. With his position in the army and connections in Delhi, he had succeeded in claiming all the land offerings the government was allocating to the victims. Even after my great-grandfather made multiple trips to Delhi to try to reconcile with his brother, the younger brother wanted nothing to do with my great-grandfather. In a last-ditch effort to sway him to come to his senses, my great-grandfather wrote his younger brother a final letter. His brother's response was: "Delhi is right here, aake fateh kar lo . . . come and conquer it." We had gone from landlords to refugees with nothing to our name.

Soon after this, my paternal grandfather was married to my grandmother, who came from a very different background, through an arranged marriage. At this time, arranged marriages were still a cultural norm. It was evident to everyone that my grandfather was not happy with this union. My grandfather was an ambitious man, while my grandmother was a humble, god-loving woman. I've always felt there was something in our family genes that caused us to never feel satisfied or fulfilled with our own lives. That sense of dissatisfaction would be transferred from my grandfather to my father and then to me. Each one of us craved a life filled with experiences, and accepting the status quo wasn't in our cards. Three generations down, we would continue to take risks, refusing to accept no for an answer. We didn't abide by the can't-do philosophy. We set out to do everything.

My grandfather escaped to Europe and then to Bangladesh, leaving family behind in Patiala—six kids and seventeen grandchildren. With the exception of one daughter, who was married off to a wealthy family in Kullu, the rest of the family continued to struggle. When I asked my grandfather what happened to his uncle and his family, I was told that they all lived a very different reality than the family he had left behind. The legacy of our family is the legacy of our people. India was conquered and invaded by Mughals, Persians, Afghanis, and the British all because we could never come together as a people and fight them as a unified nation. United we stand and divided we fall. It was only logical that I picked up a history major in addition to political science at this time in college.

Despite the odds, my father had made it to America, the land of opportunity, and it didn't matter that he hadn't become as successful as the mythical tales of many before him. The American dollar went a long way in India, and his family expected him to provide assistance to the rest who didn't have much. My Chacha ji, Dad's younger brother and the youngest of their siblings, had lost his wife at an early age to a heart attack. She left behind two young girls, Komal and Kajal. Mom had arrived in India around the same time that this tragedy had taken place, and she decided to informally adopt both of the girls under her care. In the 1980s, my younger Tayaji (Dad's second eldest brother) immigrated back to India after the Soviets invaded Afghanistan and bombed the school where he was principal. Unsurprisingly, he was a little messed up in the head from that experience. He had three children, two girls and one boy. The second child, Gurpreet, was an intelligent young woman with big dreams but no means to make them a reality. During Mom's time in India, Gurpreet also started living with her in our house in Patiala.

In order to pay for everyone's living expenses, Dad would send money to India every month, and that money was used to pay for their education. The fact was Dad was not a very rich man—he would earn around $2,000 a month, and our new home mortgage was $1,300 at an interest rate of 6 percent. When requests for money started increasing after Mom arrived in India, he would often lose his temper and be extremely frustrated by the constant pressure on him to send money. My Kabul wale Tayaji, the one who lived in Afghanistan, had paid for Dad's college back in the eighties, and so Dad returned the favor by paying for his daughters' nursing school education. During my time in college, I was the only person financially responsible for my education. Dad never asked me how much my tuition payments were or how much a college textbook cost—and because he didn't ask, I never told him how much I could have used his help. It was my ego that believed that even if no one was there for me, I could still succeed.

A few years later, my favorite teacher, Dr. Jenne from history secondary education, told me that "you can't do everything great if you have too much on your plate." I said to myself, "Watch me" and got the highest GPA of my college career even after taking twenty-four credit hours while interning on Fridays and working Saturdays and Sundays. I believed that since I had been able to get through the previous few years when no one believed I could, then what else couldn't I do? I started believing in overcoming this no-win mentality and started idolizing the role of the underdog. I knew the odds were stacked against me, but they would not break me. Whenever anyone said I couldn't do something, I took it as a challenge to prove them wrong. This mindset didn't just start in college; it had always been a part of me going back to my skating days in Karnal. When the coaches thought I wasn't going to get anywhere because of poor equipment or average skills, I gave it my all during competitions—and then some. Just like the strap-on wheels used for my skates in the 1997 Karnal City Championship, I had been dealt a bad hand in life, but like hell was I going to let that stop me from winning the gold. Naturally, I became attracted to fictional characters like Rocky Balboa from *Rocky III* and used his theme song "Eye of the Tiger" as the mentality I wanted to carry myself with. It was not only my ringtone and alarm in the morning—it was also who I was, my personal catchphrase of the decade. I had decided my life would not be defined by the decisions of others or their assumptions of what I could accomplish. However, I would continue make that mistake repeatedly and refuse to acknowledge it for many years to come.

My underdog mentality became my arrogance, and with each passing accomplishment, it cemented aspects of my behavior. Even when others offered constructive criticism, I took it personally as an insult. I had always been overly sensitive toward criticism even as a child, always trying to please everyone. Without a parent to help navigate my emotions and share my fears, I was becoming rigid in my ways. I refused to acknowledge any deficiency within myself because I perceived it to be a weakness that I could not afford during these times. I didn't have the time to stop myself and process my emotions. But if I had, I don't think I could have made it. My worldly maturity had grown because of what I had seen at such a young age, but my emotional maturity was still stuck at the age of twelve. My father suffered from these same flaws. He was unable to communicate or understand his emotions in a healthy manner, so even though he meant well deep down, his behaviors and actions came off horrifically. Being independent of having an adult figure around at the beginning of my teenage years became a handicap that I dismissed. I saw the criticism of others in the same way that my father punished me, so I would instantly become defensive. My mother was much more aware of her emotions, but she was on the other side of the world. The one time I opened up to Mom about my feelings and shared my desire to cut my hair, instead of dismissing me or thinking less of me because I wanted to separate from our religion, she was kind and listened to how I felt. She helped me process an emotion that I'd carried for so long and that manifested itself as a bull's eye for others to target me since we had come to America. But even though we had started speaking more often since I owned my own cell phone, our biggest emotional breakthrough was limited to that night. Mom had a way of reverting back to the story of her decision to leave rather than remaining in the present to witness how her son was growing. I couldn't blame her for the fact that our relationship was becoming more distant with each passing year. We were becoming very different people from who we were that day at JFK.

Ten years later, I would agree with Dr. Jenne. No matter how much you think you can handle in life, if you have too much on your plate, something will come back to bite you.

CHAPTER 10

IN 2008, THE global economy WAS on the brink of collapse. Fueled by poor lending practices and mismanagement by the top brass, the banking system as we knew it was about to be history. Sometime in the fall of my junior year, I walked into the recently renovated Guerreri student center and the TV in the middle of the room flashed with "Breaking News" headlines of the market sell-off on Wall Street, describing how politicians were holding emergency meetings on Capitol Hill to come up with a stimulus package. Little did I know that twelve years later, during the height of the coronavirus, we would get flashbacks of this period. The stock market was collapsing, and the Bush administration sent out stimulus checks to every American taxpayer trying to prop up the economy. Centre at Salisbury went from being packed seven days a week to becoming a ghost town, as if we were practicing social distancing in 2008. Stores across the mall were shutting down, and the people whom I had formed friendships with over my three years there were losing their jobs.

I depended on my commission at AT&T to make up the bulk of my pay so I could keep pace with my pending tuition payments. With the election of Maryland Governor O'Malley in 2006, tuition at state colleges had been frozen for the past two years, another coincidence in my favor. However, business fell off a cliff at the same time when we went through an ownership and management change at AT&T. Pankaj, an Indian immigrant in his late thirties with a background in hotel management, had been taking over management duties in the middle of 2008 just before the recession happened. Meanwhile, I was being recruited heavily by the owner of the Verizon kiosk who offered me eight dollars an hour plus benefits, but it felt wrong to abandon Pankaj at a time when I was the most veteran employee he was counting on to help him figure out the structure of our business. Pankaj matched the eight-dollars-an-hour offer, and we found ourselves becoming close friends during the most significant challenge to the economy since the Great Depression. Pankaj was very different from past management. He did everything the right way, even putting me on the official payroll. I was earning somewhere between $900 and $1,300 per month, though now I had to pay taxes. We were fortunate that Apple had just released a revolutionary new phone a year earlier, with exclusive rights to AT&T for five years. At first, franchise AT&T locations weren't allowed to sell the iPhone during the first year of its release, but after a coup by franchise owners, that was about to change. Even though the iPhone had a much smaller commission at the point of sale, we could still sell the customer a case, a holster, car charger, and more to make up for the lost commission.

I was never a pushy salesperson, but whenever I sold something, I formed a connection with my customer, and these relationships would keep them coming back to me year after year even when we were under competitive threats from Best Buy and Walmart and Sam's club. The most important lesson I learned during these difficult times was how important it was to form strong bonds with people. I needed them while they had other options, many of which were in their interest. However, they kept coming back to me. I learned that I wasn't just an AT&T salesperson; I had been developing business acumen for the past several years. When we ran credit checks to approve new accounts, I also realized the value of having a good credit score in order to qualify for better benefits. Through Sonya's suggestion, I discovered the website Mint.com, which helped me to manage my cash flow in a more efficient manner. I started using my line of credit almost immediately after the August tuition payment went out. First by a hundred dollars; then in September, I would be two to three hundred dollars in the hole; and in October, I cut it close to the limit at four to five hundred dollars. In November, the holiday shopping season would come to my rescue when the mall hours changed to being open for almost twenty-four hours. I would volunteer to pick up all the hours I could even if it meant less time studying for my finals. This cycle would continue each year until I graduated.

We went from two locations in the mall to just a single store location and from eight total employees to just me and Pankaj. Pankaj's wife, Karuna, worked at the Ocean City location that I switched to during my summers. My decision to stick around with Pankaj instead of taking the better job offer from Verizon earned me Pankaj's trust, and I thus managed to keep my job with continued outperformance. We became close, and Pankaj slowly learned of my background and my story. He never talked much of his own besides the fact that he had recently moved from India with his wife and two sons. He had worked for the Modi's (a highly affluent Indian family), running their flagship Thai restaurant in New Delhi, prior to coming to America. He also had experience at a management position in the Taj Mahal Palace Hotel in Mumbai, the same historic hotel that would be the target of a terrorist attack in India in November that year. Pankaj became like a father figure to me, asking about my classes and my relationship with Nicole. He was also very flexible with my hours based on my class schedule, such as when I had night sessions or needed to participate in classes during the weekend. He always encouraged me to become more active in college and to enjoy myself. He even bought me beer when I was nineteen—Miller Genuine Draft, god-awful beer. Strangely, unlike my fellow underage classmates, I was never thirsty for an older person to buy me booze. It might have been because I had always been surrounded by older guys at work since I was fifteen, and they never hesitated once to buy me alcohol. Plus, alcohol was a waste of money that I couldn't afford. I had to become an expert at money management for the sake of survival. If I missed a tuition payment, I would have to withdraw my name from school that semester.

But there was a need for balance if I was going to keep my sanity and pretend to be just like everyone else in college. After Nicole and I started dating, my social participation increased in my fraternity, and people finally started seeing me more often. I even picked up secondary education as a specialization to my history degree so I could have more classes with her. Her sorority knew who I was, and there was rarely ever a moment when I would walk on campus without someone saying, "Hey, Arjun." I wasn't invisible! But my mind was always racing faster than my feet as I tried to keep pace with my life. From the outside, things couldn't have been better, but I was struggling on the inside. I couldn't put my emotions into words or process the stress overload. When Nicole told me she was falling in love with me, I couldn't say it back; I just hugged her. A day later, I told her about my background and how I didn't want her to fall in love with me or be with me if she felt uncomfortable with my story. She decided to stay, but even though we were in love, we could never truly open up to one another. There wasn't really anyone at school I could share my struggles with as Alex had moved to attend the University of Maryland in Baltimore County and Carolyn was six hours away at the University of Virginia.

Carolyn and I had been talking almost every day since September 2006. I soon realized how problematic it was that I could talk about my issues with Carolyn instead of my girlfriend. Nicole found emails and chats of our conversations, and it made our emotional divide even larger. How could I say I was in love with Nicole when I spoke to Carolyn about my feelings in an honest way that I couldn't with Nicole? There was just something different about my relationship with Carolyn compared to anyone else who was close to me, including Alex. After Alex left for college, our friendship started fading. When she suddenly became pregnant with her ex-boyfriend's child, that trend just sped up. Our priorities shifted, and for good reason. For a mother, her child comes before anything else. But Carolyn and I were just two similar souls navigating our own personal struggles. In fact, Carolyn had no real reason to care or worry about my problems. She came from a relatively wealthy and stable background. Her dad was a partner in a law firm in town, and her family was quite well-off. They were highly educated and liberal parents who raised their children to always do the right thing. Instead of pursuing a career in lucrative fields, Carolyn chose to focus on social issues, and in some way, I was her first practical case study. In addition to our already strong friendship, my complex backstory was worthy of her attention.

I started putting together my future semester class schedules after the disaster of my freshmen year, along with the money I required almost every other week to solve the financial conundrum I found myself in. With a girlfriend came other expenses that I wasn't prepared for. The fraternity was hard enough to find money for; how was I going to pay for a fancy dinner on top of that? I don't think Nicole ever cared about those things, but I did. I didn't want to treat someone like her as though she didn't deserve the best. I was insecure about the relationship when she would go to socials with other fraternities because I didn't think I was good enough for her. I felt she could easily find someone else like her from a similar family structure and background, someone who didn't have the same baggage and continuous struggles like I did.

Relationships are complicated and hard, especially when it's your first love and you have absolutely no idea what the hell you're doing. It was my first relationship, and not having a good example of a healthy relationship in my life really put me at a disadvantage. Put someone with my background—complicated, self-doubting, egotistical, and with mommy and daddy issues—with a sweet girl from Anne Arundel's wealthy neighborhood, and voilà. What could possibly go wrong? My own unresolved emotional issues that stemmed from my separation from my mother and the big handicap of my legal status were ready to sabotage the relationship we had. In my effort to protect her or keep her from getting hurt, I became suffocating. I didn't want to lose the first person I loved like I had with my mother, but that thought itself would become a self-fulfilling prophecy. It started off strong: butterflies were flying everywhere, love was in the air, and the clouds were cotton candy; but when life became real again, everything came crashing down, hard. My immigration status would continue to reappear every year with every scholarship application that would come and go. I would write essay after essay, but without being able to apply for FAFSA, I did not qualify for any grant. There was no help coming for me, and envy started to pierce through me. Dad had lost his job two summers ago and counted on me to help with house bills. I was robbed of the opportunity to save up money for myself so that I didn't have to work so much during the semester. I kept asking myself why. What made me different from all these other people around me? I had been nine years old when we came to America. While walking the halls of Salisbury University in my Sig Pi hoodie and doing pull-ups for the Marines booth, I felt I was pretty fucking American as far as anyone could tell—only, I wasn't. I worked so much that I never had time for any campus activity. I couldn't even be a complete frat boy doing keg runs on the weekend—not that it was at the top of my to-do list, but it would have been nice to have the option.

An angry teenager is still angry even if the anger is hidden behind a smiling face. You can put on whatever face you want, but when your insides are screaming about the shitty hand you've been dealt, sooner or later, that lava will erupt and burn whoever is close enough to get hurt by the heat. Nicole broke up with me after multiple public outbursts where I embarrassed myself and her. Alcohol heightened my insecurities, and without the maturity to control my emotions, I started falling apart. I was just a boy who wanted to fit in, who wanted to be a part of something, who wanted to be with somebody I loved, who wanted to belong. But a decade had passed with no hope. I craved a normal life, even one filled with poverty or family problems, as long as I could be American. But I couldn't fix my immigration status. No matter how hard I worked, how many majors I took on in college, or how great my grades were, I could not legally work in the United States because I didn't even have a work permit. Yes, some people might say that I broke the law, but what are you supposed to do to survive? Go back to where you came from? And where is that exactly when you spent the last decade of your life becoming an American? There are more than eleven million people currently living in the United States, and they all have to do whatever they can to live and eat. When you're homeless and starving, you do whatever it takes to survive, and your concept of right and wrong will change.

As the recession worsened and more jobs were lost, I wanted to make myself more marketable in whatever future awaited me, so I picked up a business minor in my second semester of junior year with the option to pursue a Master's in Business Administration (MBA). At first, I considered pursuing law, but I remember my psychology professor telling me how her son had graduated in the top 15 percent of his class from George Washington University with a law degree but still couldn't find a job. I realized my pursuit of law school in the middle of a recession wasn't going to be the best path forward; it would be three years in comparison to two years for an MBA and a better job market. My decision at the last second of my college journey would pave the way toward my future profession.

I spent the senior year of college mourning a failed relationship, running away from my reality, spending four nights a week out drinking with my misfit friends, and feeling truly lost. I started revisiting the idea of joining the military after college—this time I could go in as an officer because I had a bachelor's degree. The problem was that even if I became an officer in the Marine Corps, it didn't guarantee citizenship for me at the end of my service. But at that point in my life, I needed direction or something greater to be a part of, rather than just being the local cell phone salesman. The act of serving our country had been passed on in my family, and it had also been part of my religion for hundreds of years. Even though she didn't consider me a part of her, my country was America. I had pledged my allegiance to the flag of the United States of America.

I stayed in my own pain for a long time. One day, I even considered driving off the Bay Bridge after I broke up with Nicole. Maybe it was fear or remembering that I still had my sister and Bibi that kept me driving straight home. From the moment I met Nicole, I had neglected my relationships with my sister, my friends, and my family. Hardeep started resenting me, and it created a wedge that couldn't be repaired as he left to attend college in North Carolina. Our bond was broken, and our relationship was limited to spending Christmas together or maybe a text message here and there whenever the Eagles played. There was only so much time in a day, and something or someone would be left out, just as Dr. Jenne, my history secondary education professor, had advised me. My affinity for history teachers had continued in college as Dr. Jenne became the first and only professor I shared my legal situation with. I always encountered the same reaction when I told people about my situation—disbelief, sadness, and empathy, even if they couldn't fully understand how this could have happened. I felt safe and comfortable talking to Dr. Jenne, especially since he specialized in social issues and had an expert understanding of historical perspective. Such things happen to people every day and has happened to millions besides me for decades, even before our current-day focus on migrant children in captivity.

During this time, my pain trumped everything, and I wasn't really there for Carolyn, either. She had been in Mexico doing a study abroad program in Merida where she fell in love with a man called Alejandro around the same time I was with Nicole. They broke up around the same time we did as well. Here we were, two broken-hearted friends caught up in our grief but able to constantly console one another. When Carolyn came back to America, I even encouraged her to return to Mexico to see if she could repair her relationship with Alex. I wanted her to give it her all to fulfill her love story. But it didn't work, and when she came back, we were all both of us had to lean on. Our own love story started as we developed romantic feelings for each other. After it became clear that neither of us was going to end up with our first love, Carolyn and I went from consoling one another to becoming inseparable. There were only so many times we could talk about what we could have done differently until the conversation turned to "What are we doing next?" With time, old wounds started to heal and clarity began to shine as we became willing to accept our grief. We all have different visions of accepting the love we think we deserve or pursuing some great love story like the one in the movie *The Notebook*, but in reality, we just need love—selfless love without expectations and a friendship that can give way to a deep understanding for one another. I knew we would always be there for each another just as we had promised years ago.

My four years in college passed by in a blink of an eye, and the end of the road was coming for me no matter how much I hid from it. All that effort to work and pay for college would never lead to a job or legal status. Who cares that I had spent fifty-six hours every week for the past four years at the mall relying on every sale to help pay for this massive feat? In the end, it would be for nothing, with no one there to understand my failure. Two majors, one honors program, and a secondary education certification complete, what could 173 credit hours give me? Nothing. Nothing was going to change, and I would spend my life living in limbo, working for one Indian business owner under the table to the next, continuously exploited. The Republicans would say I stole their jobs; the Democrats would fail to get anything done. I knew that Obama would come and go and that I would still be here, waiting for that hope his campaign slogan had promised two years before. In a desperate attempt, I started the application process for Canadian immigration. In Canada, I could become a legal immigrant based on merit, education, adaptability, employment, etc. Just as I was ready to go to a war zone four years ago, I was willing to leave everything behind again if it meant gaining my freedom—to come out of the shadows and not be ashamed of something that had never been in my control. But I would never get the chance as the worst was yet to come.

Unknown to me, for the past several years whenever I would be out late or not around the house because I was in class or at work, Sonya was being beaten by my father and told not to say a word to me. I had been blind to my sister's pain for so many years, only focused on my own selfish struggles, angry and upset with how nothing ever seemed to go right in my life. I had been present for her in only a superficial way, and I had not fulfilled my duty as her older brother to protect her from the monsters that tormented her. She had suffered over the past several years, keeping all her pain to herself. She couldn't even tell her mother over the phone because Dad was always listening in. She couldn't talk to her grandmother because a cell phone for a sixteen-year-old wasn't considered essential. She had no one to confide in, so she decided to end it all instead of continuing to suffer. On July 4, 2010, Sonya tried to overdose. She had been backing out of the driveway with the Ford Windstar when she hit my car, damaging both in the process. She was so terrified by what was going to happen to her at the hands of my dad that she decided over-dosing was better than the alternative. Luckily, she panicked after taking that step and called me to tell me what she had done. I was working in Ocean City at the time and I closed the store and sped back to Salisbury with my flashers on. I called Pankaj, who was in the Salisbury Mall, to take her to the hospital while I rushed back. I arrived in the Peninsula Regional Medical Center's emergency room, and Sonya was in the back getting her stomach pumped. Shortly afterward, Carolyn showed up, fol-lowed by Dad. Carolyn had recently graduated from UVA in the spring and had come back home for the summer to figure out her next steps. Pankaj and Karuna were also present. The mood in the hospital room was grim, caught between anger and fear. Sonya would come out of the incident fine and lie to the doctor that she had mistakenly taken too many Tylenol pills instead of telling them the truth. The truth is she never wanted to take her life—Sonya wanted to live, just not the life she had been leading for the past decade. After years of putting myself first, it shouldn't have taken me by surprise that while I was starting to live my life, my sister was suffering all alone. Just because I had attended her drama club plays and school functions or sometimes dropped and picked her up from school didn't mean I that I had been truly there for her. I told myself that something like this would never happen ever again. I had been so close to losing the only person who shared the same pains as me.

When we got back home from the hospital that night, I had already made up my mind that enough was enough. I didn't want any part of the relationship I had with my father for myself or for Sonya. We could no longer live with him. I was nervous and scared, but also angry that I had been part of the problem that had led to this situation. How could I have been so blind to what was going on? Had I been consciously ignor-ing what was going on in the background? Sonya sat next to me in the car, and I knew this time that there would be no keeping the peace; I had to fight for her. At home, I mustered up my courage and lifted my voice even though it was a bit shaky and told Dad that we were leaving him. I told him we were done, but Dad would have his say. He stood over me, trying to intimidate me. I got up and grabbed his hands and pushed him back. Sonya and I left our house in Salisbury that night without packing a single piece of clothing as Dad sat outside the front door with his head in his hands, crying. The boldest decision of my life had taken less than thirty minutes to execute. I drove my Corolla to the only place we could go—Masi's house in Dover.

The next morning, I had to go back to work in Ocean City, Maryland, so I left Sonya behind. A week later I would be fired, and a couple of days after that, someone slashed my car's tires. I would spend the next few months couch-surfing at Vincent's and Carolyn's parents' place in Salisbury. Her parents were always so kind to me. I craved for the type of mother Carolyn had, and even though Carolyn's father was a bit picky with her, he was always trying to help Carolyn see her limitless potential. Whatever I was holding on to for sanity was lost with all my hopes crushed, or so it seemed. The dramatic part of every hero's adventure comes when all hope seems lost and it looks like it can't get any worse. Just look at Frodo at the ending of *The Lord of the Rings: The Two Towers* when Sam has to give him the inspiration he sorely needs to go on. Sam tells Frodo that it is in the great tales when all hope seems lost, when everything is falling apart, how could things ever get better after so much bad had happened? It is in those tales, Mr. Frodo that the heroes go on because they were holding on to something. That there is some good in this world, and that's worth fighting for. I was desperately holding on to whatever hope my arms could reach and give me the strength to pull myself up. My parents named me Arjun after a two-week prayer ceremony in accordance to Sikh customs. Arjuna was the warrior prince from *Mahabharata*, an ancient Indian epic, representing the best aspects of humanity: courage, strength, and humility, intelligence and wisdom, commitment to truth and justice, and the performance of Dharma with Karma (Duty and Right action). Being the oldest male child in the family, that name either came with zero expectations given what our family had gone through for a generation . . . or a lot of pressure.

Sometimes you're not even the hero or your own story; perhaps someone else is. Sam is the real hero of the Lord of the Rings series, even though Frodo gets most of the credit because he carries the burden of the ring of power. I was carrying that burden too, but if it wasn't for my own Sam who would continually give me the same push to keep me moving forward, I would be finished. Sam literally picked Frodo up and took him to the heart of Mount Doom to destroy the ring, and just like that, my friend would pick me up and spark hope back into my life. My desire was not just to be successful and to make lots of money; what I wanted more than anything else was freedom. I wanted to live my life without the fear that one night, immigration agents would break into my home while I was sleeping and bag me, the nightmare I lived with for years. I crawled in a dark tunnel every night for years, hoping to find some light; but instead of the light, I would fall through an opening and keep falling until I woke up, sweating. I lived in fear even though I pretended not to let anything stop me from succeeding. Repeating the lyrics to "Eye of the Tiger" used to be a special mantra that gave me superpowers, but now even that wasn't working, I was finished, defeated, and ready to give in to the darkness that I had fought consciously for the past four years. I needed saving, and my hero, the person who loved me most, was always close by.

Carolyn proposed to me in the summer of 2010, and I said yes. For the past four years, we had shared our deepest thoughts, our fears, our dreams, and our lives. No one knew me more than her. Carolyn was my closest friend, the person who knew my every secret and my every pain. She chose to save my life, wanting nothing in return. Another Lord of the Rings moment comes into play here where the Elf queen gives Frodo the Phial of Galadriel as a light when all other lights turn to darkness. Carolyn was that light. Carolyn had a certain empathy for me that I am not sure I always deserved. Others would try to understand how I felt or console me, but Carolyn wanted to actually change my world. In our daily conversations that spanned four years, multiplied by 365 days, Carolyn grew to love me, and I loved her, too. If there was ever a person who I could hold and cry with, it was her. In my quest to be understood by the world, I won the kindest heart of them all. We got married on July 22, 2010, on her brother's birthday, at sunset by the Addy Sea in Bethany

Beach, Denver. Our wedding was small but beautiful with a few of our friends in attendance. I wish I had enjoyed that day more, but I was feeling embarrassed because Carolyn had paid for our wedding license since I was flat-out broke. It took a few months for us to figure out our living arrangement as living with my in-laws was never part of my plan. We signed a lease for a duplex in a shady part of town—it was only three hundred dollars in rent per month, so it was a start. I didn't feel comfortable with Carolyn living there, so I suggested she stay with her parents until I found a more suitable residence.

After Mom left America, I had lost my faith and given up on the idea that there was a God. But over the next few months after marriage, I recognized that I could not have made it this far if I hadn't had angels looking out for me. Whether it was getting an opportunity to work in an environment where I could sit and finish my homework, tuition increases being frozen, or the advice of my mentors, I always had someone looking out for me. My faith came back, not in terms of a religion but in terms of a higher power. Graduation was fast approaching, and I needed four As in my last semester to graduate with a 3.5 cumulative GPA to be considered an honors graduate. I had taken eighteen to twenty-four credit hours per semester since my freshman year, as well as summer and winter classes to make up for the initial screw-up. I was also in the running for graduation speaker and practiced my speech in front of my fraternity and multiple business classes before presenting it to the committee. My speech was slightly controversial, where I talked about my restored faith in a higher power rather than the "freshman 15," so I lost that opportunity. It took the final grade of my last semester to get me to the minimum GPA of 3.5000, but I did it.

Six months later, I got my green card; and two months later, I saw my mother after nine years apart.

CHAPTER 11

AFTER BEING ALMOST nine years apart, in the spring of 2011, I made my way to India to see my mom. I was finally able to travel internationally with my green card in hand. Carolyn didn't come with me because she didn't want to distract from the significance of the reunion. And Mom wasn't the only one waiting for me back in India—I would also be meeting my grandfather, grandmother, aunts, uncles, and cousins whom I hadn't seen since I was a little kid. As my flight landed in Indira Gandhi International Airport, I was confused whether the pilot had landed us in the wrong country. I had spent the previous month watching Hindi movies and preparing myself to survive twenty-one days in India . . . but this airport was way too nice for what I was expecting. Clearly, something was off. I exited the airport, and there was Mom.

She looked almost exactly the same from when we had last left her in JFK, minus a few wrinkles here and there. One thing was for sure: she definitely cried in the same way, but this time, it was tears of joy when she saw me. She was wearing a beautiful long coat and waiting directly in the center of the doorway leading out of the terminal. I was sure she had been there hours earlier to grab that spot so she wouldn't miss seeing her son. I was so excited to see her again. I was so much taller than her now, and my arms wrapped fully around her. My entire childhood had passed without seeing her, and now I was a grown man who had a mother again. After all those years spent on the phone, I had to figure out how to act around my parent. I had avoided getting scolded for all the things I had done wrong while she was away, but I had also never received a mother's comfort when I needed it the most. I was now twenty-two years old, no longer a timid twelve-year-old but a vibrant adult—patched up but still showing signs of trauma.

And so began my three weeks in India, my first time back since childhood. It felt like someone had put a virtual reality helmet on me. Just five minutes after the car drove out of the airport, I was in a different world. Along came the bikes and scooters on the road. The side of the road didn't have railings or lines or rumble strips; it was just dirt and whatever had been left over from the original asphalt pour. Slowly, more and more traffic came from all directions. I had made the grave mistake of sitting in the front. What was the driver's seat in my Toyota Corolla in the US was the shotgun seat for the passenger in India. People in India drove on the left side of the road, a legacy from its time as a British colony. The subtle reminders of colonial rule were all in plain sight, whether it was the old colonial architecture or British English being spoken around us. But even with the entrance of imported cars, metro, cell phones, and Western music and movies, as well as the consistent construction of highways and flyovers, life was different here. India was crowded—the population was fast approaching 1.3 billion people, which would rank it as the second most populated country in the world after China. There were eighteen million people alone in Delhi, the megacity capital of this emerging nation.

Mom, Baljeet, and my Mamaji (my mom's brother) had all came to the airport to pick me up. Baljeet was my Badhe Tayaji's (Dad's oldest brother's) second daughter. There was no question that we were family; she looked almost identical to Sonya. She was tomboyish in dress, appearance, and mentality, clearly made tough by the circumstances endured by women in India. You didn't want to fuck with her. My Mamaji, Mom's only brother, was a jolly man, kind and chubby. I could see the genuine love and pride in his eyes in the way he looked at me. I wasn't always the kindest toward him, which might have been influenced by my dad's disgust at his many business failures throughout the course of the past two decades. Prejudice can take hold of you even when you don't intend it to. I should have reserved my judgment because who knew what battles he was fighting? Battles against poverty, overpopulation, pollution, community, religion, and more? These were things I didn't know because I hadn't been around.

And what of poverty? My impressions of the haves and the have-nots in America didn't apply in India. My Mamaji picked me up in a Honda of some sort, which looked like a diesel version of the Honda Civic. Though I knew he wasn't a rich man, having a car in India was a big deal when you looked outside the window and saw most of the population traveling in rickshaws or scooters or bikes. Back when we lived in India, we didn't even have a car; the four of us would be packed together on one motorcycle. Though this would be a safety issue in America, in India, that was the way of life. I looked out on the road and saw many families just like mine doing what we had done a decade and a half ago. I felt like keeping my eyes closed while we were on the road or risk having a panic attack from the number of times we almost crashed into someone else. When we made our way through Delhi to get to where we would be staying, we went through some unpaved streets with potholes that could fit an entire car. Our flat unit was a nice place that belonged to Mom's family friend, a high-level government official. If you looked out to the street and then considered the level of respect these people commanded in their respective fields, it felt jarring. Shouldn't they be living in a better neighborhood? The flat was large, with four bedrooms and three bathrooms and a well-sized living room and common area, but the street it was on was narrow and old, just a block down from the flyover for the Delhi Metro. The idea of wealthy neighborhoods wasn't a clear concept in this part of Delhi, though they were appearing quickly in the new expansion cities of Gurgaon and Noida.

The rest of my trip in India would become a constant reminder of how good I had it in America, even during the worst of days. In America,

I wasn't in the middle of eighteen million people in one city trying to make something of my life. I had a car at the age of sixteen; all the apartments we had lived in had central air; and access to hot water or a shower wasn't a foreign concept. Whatever I wanted to accomplish, I could do it quickly and move on to the next task instead of being stuck in a traffic jam for hours in order to travel ten miles. I could fly anywhere in the country by driving two hours to Baltimore/Washington International Airport or three hours to Dulles International Airport. It took us six hours to travel from Delhi to Patiala, and the road trip didn't come with a plethora of welcome centers, gas stations, or drive-throughs. India was under construction, and every few miles there would be a detour of off-roading until the highway appeared again. There was so much dust in the air that I had to keep covering my face to breathe.

After a long six-hour road trip on under construction highways, we reached our house in Patiala. In the early part of the new millennium, my parents had started sending all their money to India to build a house in Patiala, which finished construction after Mom arrived. There was an empty lot right next to the house filled with garbage from the neighborhood—sorry, waste management wasn't coming around every Monday morning to pick up trash. The neighbor behind our house had those old-school cow-poop circles all over the side of the house that were used as fuel for stoves and heat. Our family lived within ten minutes of each other. My Badhe Tayaji had a townhouse-type property with one bedroom on the lower level past the living room. You had to go through the living room in order to get to the bedroom, similar to a railroad apartment. The second level housed my grandfather and another room that I assume was for their four kids. The third level had a new room built for paying guests or renters. My younger Tayaji lived in a one-room apartment with his wife and three children, sponsored by a foreign family so they could live and eat. My Chachaji lived in a one-room house, the location of his own business where he had set up video game rentals in his living room for the local kids, with the income helping him to meet his needs. It was like going to a Dave & Buster's, but if Dave and Busters was the size of three TVs in a small room with people playing Call of Duty, Gran Turismo, and Mario.

Meanwhile, Mom lived in our house, which had three bedrooms along with two bathrooms on the lower level alone, as well as a large living room, kitchen, common area, and a foyer leading to the second level. The foyer was almost like an indoor veranda where someone on the second floor could come out of the bedroom and look down on the dining room and kitchen. There were four additional bedrooms and bathrooms on the second level, along with an outdoor rooftop. The third level was the roof, which was also accessible if you really wanted to be alone. The bathrooms were built for royalty, with toilet seats made from artisanal woodwork. There were showers and bathtubs larger than any I had seen in America. The house had recessed lighting outside on the second level, and my room was large enough to be considered two rooms, with a walk-in closet and private bathroom. It didn't take me very long after arriving in Patiala to realize that I didn't just have it good in America; I had it good everywhere. I had worked all throughout college to pay for my monumental tuition bill, but my cousin Gurpreet didn't have the same opportunity to work at her local mall's AT&T store in India to pay for her education. The notion of upward mobility is a fallacy in certain parts of the world. The efficiencies, access, and freedom, as well as the tools available, in America are light years ahead of what some people live with in other parts of the world.

It was also at this time that I truly appreciated what my father had done. I realized that my life was what it was because of the decisions he had made for his family. I may never forgive him for what he did to Sonya in the midst of his struggles, but I gained back some respect for him. Dad and I had barely spoken for a year after what had happened. But when he found out that I had gotten my green card and that I was headed to India, he told Mom to spare no expense to welcome me. When I saw the state the rest of my family was living in, I finally understood why Dad had made the decision to take his family to America, even if he had never explained his reasons explicitly. It took me fourteen years to start putting the puzzle pieces together of who my father was. Our relationship would continue to be complicated, but I no longer felt hatred in my heart toward him. He never apologized for the things he had done, but I understood that it was difficult for him to express his shame. I respected him and the sacrifices he continued to make for the people he knew he may never see again.

CHAPTER 12

WHEN I RETURNED to America, it was back to work in Salisbury. Back to figuring out the next step. Looking for the next hurdle to cross. Even with my legal status troubles in the rearview mirror, the pot of gold was missing. I had no parent or guardian around. I couldn't bring Mom back with me yet; I had to become a US citizen first. And everyone else was gone. Dad had left for Connecticut to work shortly after the ER overdose incident, and Sonya was living with Masi in Dover. My best friend, Vincent, was leaving for Austin to get away from small-town Salisbury and move on with his life. After a few months of struggling in the slums of Salisbury, I realized the best option for Carolyn and me to live together would be moving back into Dad's old ranch house. Though Carolyn and I lived together, things started changing. We were no longer friends but had to learn how to exist as husband and wife. She completed her degree in Latin American studies with full honors, but there wasn't a big job market available in that section of the economy for a recent graduate unless she moved to DC as an unpaid intern. She became frustrated and started working at Vernon Powell, a local shoe store in Salisbury, as a salesperson. The worst days of the recession were behind us, but the unemployment rate for recent college graduates was over 18 percent. Both of us were left searching for answers.

Whoever posted those salary figures back in Mr. Kessler's AP Psychology class must have been smoking some serious crack, because I was out of college and not making the promised fifty to sixty thousand dollars a year. The country was emerging from the worst recession since the Great Depression, and recovery was slow to come to the Eastern Shore. I applied to every job I could find on CareerBuilder, Monster, LinkedIn, and Salisbury University's placement website, and none of them would email me back. Success wasn't just going to happen because I had made it out of college with multiple degrees and no debt. I couldn't eat my degrees, and those degrees didn't pay royalties. When I was pursuing my undergraduate studies in college, I knew I had to complete a certain number of prerequisites and classes to get my major. I knew I had to work a certain amount of hours to pay for a set amount of expenses. But all of that was now over. It was time to find new motivation to make something of myself even if I didn't have a clear goal in mind. This would soon take the shape of spending hours in the library studying for the GMAT.

My first go at the GMAT didn't really put up a respectable score. It was enough to get me accepted into the MBA program at Salisbury University, but I wanted the small-school distinction to stop following me. I wanted a Georgetown, a Harvard, or even a University of Maryland degree on my wall. It seemed like everyone had left Salisbury, and I was back to swimming in a small pond, being another small fish. I was faced with the upcoming August session for MBA classes to start at Salisbury or a summer spent in the library studying for the GMAT to improve my score. The next year and half would pass in limbo as I figured out what I planned to do. I had little direction, minus the desire to add the MBA abbreviations at the end of my name. I spent a lot of my time in the library, studying GMAT textbooks to raise my score or writing essays to my top-choice schools. I would complete applications that would never be sent because I feared rejection or my inability to afford the costs. When I attended a multi-college MBA tour held in Arlington, Virginia, I finally realized that I couldn't afford to pay for a hefty MBA degree from an NYU or a Georgetown years after I graduated even if I landed a six-figure job. It was a risk I didn't deem worthy taking on, and so I decided to stick around in Salisbury.

I landed a job at Enterprise a few months into my evening MBA program and made a whopping $13.50 an hour as a management assistant, a fancy word for their car cleaning insurance salesmen. If there was ever a way to take advantage of recent college graduates, Enterprise mastered it. In the name of a fancy management assistant title, you would make less than thirty thousand dollars a year working five and a half days a week, and all the damage waivers you sold came with zero commission. But hey, who gives a shit? I was the number one employee in the entire DC region three months into the job. I would sell the crap out of those damage waivers if it meant being promoted into management. I started working part-time at my old AT&T job so my friend Pankaj could go home early to his kids; plus, I needed the extra money to pay for the MBA.

Meanwhile, things were getting quite uncomfortable at home with Carolyn. We fought frequently because of the dirty dishes, how messy the house was, or some other stupid reason that allowed us to vent our frustrations. We both had worked so hard to get to this point, and we both deserved more from life than the emotional distress in the early days of us being together twenty-four seven. I had never lived with a significant other before. After establishing an initial diplomacy, in which I moved aside for Carolyn's wants, that arrangement faded and her requests started to feel like constant nagging. I had thought we were so similar, yet when it came to living in the same house, it felt like we were at war, fighting battles over chores or furniture or what to watch on television. I could never have imagined how hard it would be to adjust to living with another strong personality, where compromise seemed next to impossible. When we fought, she became irritable with me, and our voices grew louder with each passing argument. She also felt like I was holding her back from pursuing her career to become a US ambassador one day. The love we once shared seemed like it was quickly fading away. Carolyn started having second thoughts about her decision to be with me. With regard to her past efforts to support my cause, she felt like she had made the worst decision of her life.

Our first year together was so tough that we were in danger of never speaking to each other again, with both parties blaming the other for their misfortunes. Add in the fact that we weren't doing well financially—we hadn't been out to eat in months—and it was like lighter fluid on our troubles. We started avoiding each other until, one day, I confronted Carolyn to ask why she was so upset with me. I loved her so much, but I never wanted her life to be impacted negatively on my account. Why did she blame me for ruining her life when it had been her decision to propose to me? Did she no longer feel the same love she once had for me? In the end, we decided to separate for a little while in the hopes of saving the friendship we once shared. When Carolyn was accepted into the foreign service program at Georgetown University, she left for DC. It was the number one program for that field in the world, and nobody deserved it more. I wasn't going to hold her back just because I still needed her at home. We would always be partners, and our paths were forever connected no matter what happened; but we also both deserved love from someone else in a much different way.

Just like that, two years of my life flew by with nothing of relevance. I spent my days working and my nights in classes or in the mall babysitting the store while completing my coursework. Carolyn and I were happier apart than we were together, and we picked up our old form of communication via Google Chat and weekend trips up to Georgetown. There wasn't much nightlife in Salisbury outside of college, and my friends had all left town, so I wasn't interested in partying anyway. My biggest struggle in life was over, but what had I achieved? A broken family separated by states and continents. An empty house with no love or joy. Luckily, Sonya was accepted to Salisbury University and she soon returned to Salisbury after living with Masi for the past year, a welcomed event. President Obama had just issued DACA, Deferred Action for Childhood Arrivals, as an executive order, which would allow Sonya to attend public university or college with in-state tuition so she wouldn't have to lie about her immigration status, which was still pending. But alas, there were still no scholarships or grants available for the woman who had been four years old when she was brought to this country. The DACA executive order brought a ton of heat down on Governor O'Malley from the right, but what was so wrong with that executive order? On June 18, 2020, the Supreme Court ruled in favor of DACA; meanwhile, over two hundred thousand of those same DACA kids or dreamers are serving on the frontlines in the battle against COVID-19, with close to thirty thousand of them in the medical field. Yet the ruling was more along technicalities rather than a sense of empathy for these dreamers. They are still waiting for a path to citizenship and a way out of the limbo. The Supreme Court ruling was a step in the right direction but it is not even close what must be done and done now. It has been almost two decades of the "Dream Act" stalling in Congress through three administrations and neither party has done anything but give false hope. These people want nothing more than to belong to the only country they have ever known, yet they are waiting from one administration to the next for action. There was nothing I could do for Sonya or my mother for now. I just did my best to guide my sister however I could. In time, she would find her own path and make her own set of sacrifices, but she wouldn't have to do it alone—her big brother would always be there for her.

Sonya was a much different person than the girl who almost ended her life a year ago. In the past year, she had seen a glimpse of the life that Masi gave her children—a house full of love and acceptance, with Bibi right there to nurse her mental health back to recovery. Bibi was the strongest person I knew. She didn't fear or second-guess anything. She had spent her entire life at the service of her family and had been the foundation of the patriarchal household, even though she wasn't in the role at the top. I always wished that I could be more like her and that I could have had the same chance as Sonya to be around her after everything that happened with Dad. Years later, Sonya would tell me how Hardeep, Amanjot, and Masi would all huddle around in Masi's master bedroom, just laughing and talking, and how alone that made Sonya feel. Even though she was with a family who loved and cared for her, she was still an outsider. We would both talk about how Masi never had a single picture of us in her house even while we both craved to be part of her family. Sonya missed her senior year in high school after she left Salisbury and started taking classes at the local community college to finish her high school education and also gain some college credits. When she came back to Salisbury a year later, she started dating her best friend's brother, Quintin, and fell in love with him. I never liked the guy—he never spoke much in front of me, and I always thought that he was hiding something. I didn't trust his intentions with my sister. I finally knew what it felt like to be playing the part of a father figure.

The hardships we endured hardened our resolve but not our soul. The desire for love and the warmth of family would remain unfulfilled in me for a long time to come. My success at work was necessary in light of the responsibility my family had placed on my shoulders. If I didn't succeed, I wouldn't meet the income qualifications necessary to apply for a green card application for Mom as an immediately family member. And if I didn't succeed, then why had I worked so hard in college? If I didn't succeed, then would I ever get to enjoy the life I had sorely missed living? I knew I would have to succeed.

On Thanksgiving weekend in 2012, I sent a LinkedIn application for a job opening at Morgan Stanley in Annapolis, Maryland. Two hours later, my application was picked up by Warren Wright, assistant complex director in Washington, DC. Two days later, I had a phone interview with the branch manager in Annapolis. And two days after that, I had my face-to-face interview, with a job offer faxed to me the next day. Within a week of applying for the position, I had left Salisbury and relocated to Annapolis, the state capitol two hours away. I guess answering the interview question "How much do you know about Morgan Stanley?" by saying "I have seen the movie *The Pursuit of Happyness*" was a good answer. Dean Witter, the firm Chris Gardner would eventually work for, was acquired by Morgan Stanley in the late 1990s. I was a part of the Morgan Stanley Financial Advisor Associate class of December 2012, and one year later I was in the top tier of their financial advisor associates (FAAs). Through the two-hour car rides after work to MBA classes in Salisbury and my midnight return journey to Annapolis, from the right shoulder pain I would develop from appendicitis to the days and nights spent cold calling investment clients, I was going to be successful. I wanted to be successful as badly as I wanted to breathe. Clear eyes, full hearts, can't lose.

I had found my calling. This had always been my path—I'd made it through the crazy squiggly-line journey of life that had brought me to my current position as a financial advisor. Life had taught me more about money and wealth management than anything I could have learned in school. In turn, I had a desire to teach and help people with money management, which was what I knew and did best. To have an opportunity to work in a career not constricted by a cap but with the ability to grow as much as I wanted and to earn as much as my work dictated was the true symbolism of capitalism. I was finally going to be rewarded by my success and work ethic. My family had suffered through financial hardships in addition to immigration issues, which only amplified that struggle. If I could help a family plan for their children's future education, give them a sense of comfort that their decisions would not lead to financial ruin, and provide them with a peace of mind so that their household would not suffer the same battleground as mine, it would be the greatest reward of them all. Every obstacle in my past had led me to this end. Every failure had taught me a lesson for the future. This was what I was meant to do—to help the most amount of people in the best way I could.

I became a US citizen in May of 2014 with only my dad and Pankaj in the audience. My relationship with Carolyn was strained to the point where her priorities had shifted to herself and grad school, and she couldn't come to my oath ceremony. We were talking again, but she still blamed me for holding her back. But that never changed my view of her; I will forever hold her dear to me. Not just because she made my citizenship possible, but because even if I hadn't had an immigration issue, I still couldn't have imagined my life without her. It's funny how one document can be so important to allowing you to finally feel like you belong. The coveted citizenship to the United States of America was mine. I was free; I was officially part of a community that I had always thought of as my home. Although I could never become president, I could finally call myself an American and it wouldn't be a lie. After a few beers with Pankaj and my other best friend, Vinh, the first thing I did was file a petition for Mom. It would take a year and a half of getting through Indian bureaucracy to get her documents in order before the petition could be reviewed. But her time was coming.

CHAPTER 13

I PLANNED MY next trip to India in a way that would enable me to stop by London. London was the city I had dreamed of seeing since the first time I'd seen the movie *Dilwale Dulhania Le Jayenge* when I was a little boy. London, the capital of the British Empire that had ruled over India for centuries, figured large in my imagination. And the trip didn't disappoint. The city was as great, if not greater, than my wildest dreams. The big bus tour helped me see the whole city in less than twelve hours, and the sunset boat ride at the end wasn't too shabby, either. My timing couldn't have been better with the city decorated for Christmas—even Big Ben and the London Eye joined in the seasonal cheer by being lit up in green and red.

My plane landed in Delhi in a cloud of smog. I couldn't have been more sleep deprived to start my few days in India. This trip was the result of the news that December 15, 2015, was the date that would decide Mom's fate for the fourth and final time. After multiple previous attempts had failed to get Mom back to America, this was her last hope, and I had planned a trip to India to make sure it would go through. The problems started piling up the Friday before the interview when someone from the US embassy called to confirm Mom's appointment on the 15th at 8:30 a.m. The person reminded us that we needed to have her fingerprints done in Delhi before the appointment. Too bad they hadn't told us this beforehand, and we were six hours northwest of Delhi at the time in Chandigarh, my birthplace, visiting Mamaji. So began a three-hour back-and-forth phone call between me and the embassy employees who couldn't or wouldn't set up the biometric fingerprinting appointment. After multiple times of being hung up on or the network being lost, we finally got Mom scheduled for fingerprinting on December 14, a day before the interview. We were supposed to spend a few days in Patiala, but now everything had to be rushed. Once we reached home, my paternal grandfather, who had been at odds with Mom over some family conflict, finally came to join the family. He had moved back to India after he could no longer live on his own as he was fast approaching ninety years of age. In those few hours, I was able to start a FaceTime call with my grandfather and Dad—they hadn't spoken in three years—to reconcile the broken relationship between my grandfather and Mom. I think he relented as a way of sending off Mom to America even though the outcome of her visa interview was still to be determined.

We went back to Delhi a day before the interview for the fingerprinting appointment. We had not made a reservation on the premium Volvo bus, so the regular desi bus it was. After a six-hour bus ride meant for much smaller people who didn't have my frame, with two people per seat that looked like it had been designed for children, we finally arrived. In my mind, the hardest part of this whole interview process would be getting my passport back in time for my return flight on December 17 so I could attend Sonya's graduation on December 19, but what I didn't realize was the interview was going to be the toughest part.

We arrived at the embassy at 8 a.m. on December 15 for an 8:30 a.m. appointment. After following a procedure similar to that at the DMV in the US, we finally got to the immigration officer. When we reached her window, she looked at me and knew I was the petitioner. She told me she was going to interview my mom alone and asked me to sit back down. I stood diagonally apart from Mom and told her I was right there as I

TEARS IN THE FLAG

saw the fear overwhelming her face. During the process, the officer asked questions that had nothing to do with her being the mother of a US citizen. Instead, the questions were more along the lines of her original time in America and why, after she had left the country, she didn't try to return to her kids. Why did she overstay her visa? Why had she left? What could have been more important than staying with her children? Why didn't she try harder to get back? She then proceeded to ask questions about how I became a citizen. When and how did your son meet his wife? She was trying to poke holes through my own immigration case. She used basically every single scare tactic she could have used. I thought about calling Carolyn and putting her on speakerphone to knock some sense into this woman. I think she assumed that I was uneducated or unaware of my rights and easily swindled. After fifteen to twenty minutes of this grilling, she asked Mom to sit down.

When she called us back to the window a second time, I walked up with Mom. I explained to the officer, "I didn't travel halfway across the world to sit and watch." She let me stand beside Mom but wouldn't let me answer any questions. When I tried to clarify an answer, she told me to sit back down again, which I did, visibly frustrated, and I verbally expressed my disgust. She continued asking Mom similar questions. A few minutes later, she called me up to inform me that she was going to put Mom's case on hold. "Why?" I asked. She explained that it was because of the answers Mom had provided. Apparently, a hardship waiver had been filed and denied back in 2004. Even Senator Joe Biden had written a letter to allow Mom to return. If that was the case, why had that request been denied? The fight wasn't over yet. I told her that the waiver was before my time and asked why the document hadn't been listed as a requirement for supporting documentation prior to the interview. The woman responded by saying that I should have gotten an attorney. "An attorney for what?" I asked. "Is there any question that she is my mother? That she has completed her ten-year ban from reentering the United States and then some? What's the problem?" She responded that the waiver would explain if there had been a legal reason (such as money laundering, smuggling, etc.) that the case was denied. She added, "I have already spent fifteen minutes with you, and I have sixty-seven other people to interview." I replied, "My mom hasn't seen my sister for almost fourteen years. I think you can make more time. You have frightened my mom, and everyone else here is freaked out because of how you're speaking." She finally said, "Sit back down and talk to my supervisor." We returned to the seating area. In my mind, I was already coming up with possible defenses and answers based on whatever the supervisor might ask. Mom had started crying and shaking, and I kept reassuring her that everything was going to be fine. They couldn't use a letter before my time as a reason to put the case on hold. If it was really that big of an issue, it would have been brought to our attention when we first received the interview notice. I was confident that I would get this accomplished.

The supervisor called us up shortly afterward. I started off by saying, "Ma'am, it is completely wrong to use a letter from the now–vice president as a reason to keep my mom's case on hold." As I kept talking, she just smiled and finally said, "Congratulations, your case has been approved. Your mom will receive her green card on arrival in the US." I was awestruck. What had just happened? The supervisor was a blond woman, maybe a few years older than me, and she hadn't asked a single question. The funniest part? I had only applied for a family-based visa; I had not filled out the form I-485 for adjustment of status for a green card. Getting a visa alone would have been a victory, but being approved for a green card felt like a cruel joke, as if it was a mistake that would later be withdrawn. I often wondered later about this turn of events. Had I been watched by someone behind the glass or the camera the entire time? Was it because of how adamant I had been? There I was, a twenty-six-year-old brown kid raising a ruckus in the morgue-like environment of the US Embassy. Someone had clearly noticed. Or had it been another angel sent to help me win a battle that had eliminated many others before me? I couldn't understand what happened and failed to fully react with enthusiasm because good things usually didn't happen to me. Till today, I still struggle with expressing gratitude whenever something extraordinary happens to me because of a lifetime of disappointment. But this moment wasn't one of them. After three hours at the embassy, Mom got on the phone, calling up one person after another to let them know what had happened. She looked like a politician letting her constituents know she had gotten something done. She was in as much disbelief as I was.

What had originally seemed like the more difficult part of getting her passport back in time and finding an available seat on the flight to America came easy over the next two days. The passport, which was supposed to take three to seven days to process, only took one day and was available for pickup. And there was a ticket available on the same two flights from Delhi to London and from London to DC, so Mom even got to see London.

But the biggest surprise wasn't until the day after we arrived in the US. My sister was graduating with her bachelor of science, the first one in our family with a BS instead of a BA. I didn't tell anyone that Mom was coming back with me. It was a beautiful, sunny December day. At the entrance of the Civic Center where the graduation ceremony was being held, Mom and Dad reunited for the first time in years. I think everyone couldn't believe that this day had finally became a reality. Sonya, unaware of all this, had gone ahead to sit with her classmates. Her hair was curled, and she was wearing a beautiful white dress underneath her gown. I wanted to tell her that Mom was here the moment I saw her, but I held it in even though I was sure she could see right through me. She knew I was hiding something, but I didn't want to take the surprise of this moment away from her. This was her day in every way, and I wanted her to feel on top of the world. I was so proud of her, and I couldn't think of a better graduation gift than to reunite her with Mom. A little while into the graduation ceremony, Sonya looked back into the audience and texted me: "Who is that sitting next to Dad?" I didn't respond. After the ceremony, I went downstairs to receive her and started recording with my video camera . . . after a two-minute walk back to us, my sister finally saw her mother again after thirteen years, five months, and four days.

CHAPTER 14

IN 1492, THE Italian explorer Christopher Columbus "discovered" the New World, even with millions of people already living there. I guess he discovered this New World for Europeans when he stumbled on the Bahamian Islands and started a three-century-long genocide and extermination of the native population of the Americas. His fellow explorers landed in Jamestown, Mexico, and each of them brought with them disease, guns, and death. As the world would come to find out in 2020, disease can be far more powerful than weapons. The immune systems of the Native Americans had never been exposed to diseases from the West, and they failed to combat the dual onslaught of disease and gunpowder. One could argue that the people living in the Americas were considered "savages" and that the Europeans brought them a civilized way of life, an excuse used for centuries to justify the massacre and looting. But at the same time, Europe had yet to see any semblance of peace on its own shores. The European continent was under a constant state of warfare because of wars of territories or religious differences. Who were they to judge someone as civilized or savage?

The colonial forces would establish their provinces and colonies by the coast and then slowly start penetrating further inland until the entire continent came under their control. It wouldn't be until after the Civil War almost 350 years later that the entirety of the Union Army would be launched against what was left over of the Native American tribes, thus completing the conquest of America. In US history and world history taught in the 2000s, we would study the demise of the Aztec and Incan Empire but with little to no details of what happened in modern-day America. One chapter would be dedicated to the Trail of Tears and westward expansion, and the rest of the time period would be summarized by focusing on manifest destiny and men like Teddy Roosevelt. Whatever happened to the people now restricted to a few small reservations and casinos across the land? Why was it much easier to talk about the Holocaust or the Ukrainian famine post-WWII rather than recognizing the dirty American history swept under the rug?

The early immigrants to the New World were criminals. They were people seeking religious freedoms, hunting for riches, or just exiled from Europe. But as things started to stabilize and the threat of those pesky Natives died down, immigration exploded. The land of opportunity was born, and no one had to be under the thumb of some king or monarch. The early colonists needed help getting set up in the New World—building houses and plantations and working the fields—so they sponsored the journey of others from Europe over to the New World in return for their services to them for a number of years. This wasn't necessarily the birth of indentured servitude as it was a similar concept to being a squire for a knight or an apprentice for a blacksmith for a number of years before you became a professional yourself. But the problems started when the trusted intern, apprentice, or indentured servant was released from their commitment to landowners, and now landowners needed to figure out how else to get the labor they needed to run the plantation. Enter slavery.

America transitioned from using indentured servants in the sixteenth century to relying on the cheaper and longer-lasting alternative of slavery in the seventeenth century. When a colonist bartered for an indentured servant, the relationship came with an expiration date; but when they bought a slave, they owned that person for life—they even owned their children and their children's children, thus removing the necessity of purchasing labor. Slavery would become the foundation of America for over two hundred years and will be forever remembered in our history. From the Three-Fifths Compromise to the Civil War, history and Hollywood has revisited this era over and over again even as new forms of slavery continue to this very day. But during this time period, slavery mostly consisted of kidnapping Africans and shipping them across the Atlantic to be sold in slave markets across the Americas. With it came a consistent supply of cheap labor of over twelve million people kidnapped from their homes and sold off to work in plantations, do construction, perform housework, and whatever other labor their masters demanded of them. These were people sold off to another person for five or ten dollars in the 1700s to live and work in the most grotesque environments to build the backbone of a new nation, with no hope that they would ever become free. It's not like there wasn't any slavery in Europe at the time, but the demand was high in the New World, and vast fortunes were to be made by the slave traders. The end of slavery in France came around in 1794 when France abolished it for the first time after the French Revolution, only for Napoleon to bring it back in 1802, but the winds of change were rising. The abolitionists were gaining ground in America and the Underground Railroad was born. The Civil War came, and with it a couple of reasons: Was the war for states' rights versus federal government, or was it for abolishing slavery? Which one was it? Let's just say this to some of my AP US History teachers from Parkside High School or those who argue that the Civil War was more about states' rights—why start a civil war over that? Lincoln, the man who kept the Union together, made a great speech about how all men were created equal, reiterating what was written in the Constitution. Today, he is remembered as the man who kept the Union together and put an end to slavery, not as the president who ruled with an iron fist ignoring the rights of state governments. The reason why the Articles of Confederation (the first government system in America) failed in the first place was because of the greater powers given to the states compared to that of the federal government, and thus the

Constitution was born to give authority to both the federal and state governments. But even if the Civil War brought an end to slavery, we failed to give equal rights to those new citizens. They were freed but not equal, and the infamous Jim Crow laws were born.

After the official reconstruction, Southern states adopted Jim Crow laws to maintain segregation, denying certain benefits to the new citizens. Voting, the greatest power of individual citizens to make their voices heard, was under attack by the Southern Democrats, and thus continued the tradition of keeping the Black population suppressed. Something I have often thought of when studying history is that even 150 years after the end of slavery, the Black population continues to struggle socioeconomically. Why is that? Could it be due to the lack of opportunities since the birth of America? The social injustices they suffered even after freedom? Or the current racism still prevalent today in TikToks, the display of rebel flags, and the guns of police officers? Similar arguments could be made of what's happened in Africa, the Middle East or India—would they still be so poor or conflict-ridden if not for the lasting legacy of colonial powers? When people are imprisoned, denied citizenship, and have their resources taken from them by those with bigger guns, do they suffer for many generations as a result of these injustices? I will leave you to answer those questions.

It wasn't until the civil rights movement that Black and minority Americans finally cemented the concept that separate is inherently unequal. This brings us to modern-day America, where cheap labor has to come from somewhere else. There are over eleven million illegal immigrants currently living in the United States. You have seen many of them as farm workers, janitorial staff, and Uber drivers; or in restaurant kitchens, convenient stores, and maybe even your very own AT&T cell phone store. These are the people who make up the modern-day labor force of America. Gone are the days of indentured servants or slavery, but here are the days of exploiting illegal immigrants, as I once was. In 2012, President Barack Obama passed an executive order to allow the children of illegal immigrants to work legally in the United States or finally get the opportunities denied to them from the mistakes of their parents. Mistakes like leaving their home and families behind in search of a better future for their children in America. When Congress didn't address the issue fast enough, the president used his authority of executive action to provide a path forward. The arguments of executive overreach would spread throughout Fox News, the Tea Party, and Republicans constituents like wildfire, but no one remembered that it was actually President Bush who first proposed congressional action on the Dream Act five years before. How much time does Congress need exactly to pass one good piece of legislation? How many families and children suffer as a result of their consistent laziness or pretend bickering? These people are running away from gangs or poverty at home to sacrifice their lives for hope in the land of opportunity.

Immigration policy in America is just one modern-day example of the oppression of a group of people. We know immigrants are here and have been here for most of their lives, but we still deny them the basic rights and opportunities to excel and work their way up the ladder. There are a few ways to get a green card in the United States. The most popular way is getting married to a US citizen, the second is getting sponsored by a company making more than five hundred thousand dollars a year in revenue, the third is being a family member of a US citizen, and the fourth is if you're an asylum seeker. That's about it. The second and fourth methods can take years, if not a decade, to be processed. Meanwhile, Canada's immigration system is based on merit, such as education, language skills, work skills, and adaptability, among others. After you come to the United States as a child, or as refugees jumping the border, as is the stereotype of illegal immigrants, there aren't many options to ever become legal, and thus begins the oppression and exploitation. To this day, Sonya is still on the DACA program with no prospects of becoming legal anytime soon. She has started her application process to immigrate to Canada just like I did in 2010. If America refuses to give these children their due, they will leave, and this will lead to the brain drain that saps the innovation from this country.

In 2020, an eighteen-year-old illegal immigrant may work seventy-two hours a week to earn a wage of less than six dollars an hour in cash with no benefits because they have no other option. The employer saves money on taxes and gets cheap labor, and the eighteen-year-old gets a job that some might argue they should be grateful for or that they don't deserve. That's the same thing people said a hundred years ago after slavery ended. First there was prejudice against immigrants like the Irish, the Italians, the Eastern Europeans, and the Jews; now it's the Arabs, the Mexicans, and the Asians. What's changed in three hundred years? We continue to vilify those seeking opportunity and escaping persecution because they don't look like us, they don't talk like us, and they don't believe in the same God as us. In reality, they have come to the country in the same way as every American's ancestor, but we refuse to accept this because it's easier to point a finger at things we don't understand. This is the modern-day fight for equal rights for every man, woman, and child who risked it all for a chance at a better life. We may not have a Martin Luther King or an Abraham Lincoln in our corner, and our last champion has already served his two terms as president, but we have the ability to have our voices heard through social media. We are here; we are Americans, too; and we are not going anywhere.

Is America the land of opportunity or the country that is so desperately trying to maintain its grip of being number one that it would rather let the invisible continue to suffer just to keep pace with the Chinese? The people without a voice or rights who continue to pick up the trash and grow the crops to keep this country fed in the midst of a global crisis deserve more. Many of the largest companies in the world were founded by American immigrants—this is the version of America that has attracted millions across the globe. The city on the hill is such because it's the land of opportunity, and our strength is in our diversity, our resilience, and our innovation, which must be held to a higher standard. Just like that day at the American embassy in New Delhi that was filled with terrified people, this country is filled with people who can't speak up or who refuse to because it may bring negative attention upon them. Being terrified of losing what they had sacrificed to achieve is why no one will come forward to address the pains of their present-day suffering.

After Mom came back, I felt like Frodo at the end of *The Lord of the*

Rings: The Return of the King when he walks around in the Shire, having just finished writing *The Lord of the Rings*. He recites, "How do you pick up the threads of an old life? How do you go on, when in your heart you begin to understand . . . there is no going back? There are some things that time cannot mend. Some hurts that go too deep, that have taken hold." No green card can bring back the thirteen years spent apart from a parent, the years of living in fear of being bagged and dragged away by ICE agents in the middle of the night. Mom missed our childhood, and she only saw us again when we had become adults. Today we are a family in pictures alone; our differences are that of time lost. A husband who saw himself become an old man waiting for the wife he never thought he would see again, whose case file has become so thick with his past mistakes that who knows when and if he will ever become a legal resident of this country. A child who lost her mother to a manmade border, unable to cross it for the fear of never being able to come back or else be exiled to a country she has no memory of. My sister still lives with that fear, knowing that at any moment her time in this country may come to an abrupt and sudden end. Will you not speak up for her? Does she not deserve more? Will America rise to the occasion or fall backward? That much is up to you.

CPSIA information can be obtained
at www.ICGtesting.com
Printed in the USA
LVHW092057300920
667476LV00008B/635

9 781977 231833